Riding the Tail of the Dragon

By

Jeannine Dahlberg

12.20.02
To Martha
Enjoy the Ride!
Jeannine Dahlberg

This book is a work of fiction. Places, events, and situations in this story are purely fictional. Any resemblance to actual persons, living or dead, is coincidental.

© 2002 by Jeannine Dahlberg. All rights reserved.

No part of this book may be reproduced, stored in a retrieval system, or transmitted by any means, electronic, mechanical, photocopying, recording, or otherwise, without written permission from the author.

ISBN: 1-4033-4507-4 (e-book)
ISBN: 1-4033-4508-2 (Paperback)

Library of Congress Control Number: 2002108210

This book is printed on acid free paper.

Printed in the United States of America
Bloomington, IN

1stBooks - rev. 10/14/02

To my daughters Heidi and Erika,
who encouraged me to tell my story,
And
to my brother Fred, a Renaissance man,
who always will be my mentor.

CHAPTER ONE

It's difficult to explain what the fascination is with the old Ramsey place. It isn't pretty anymore. Green ivy wraps around its exterior structure leaving only the windows to reflect its character, which is reminiscent of a stately mansion. Massive foliage from giant oak trees and thick moss hang heavily over the roof cutting off all chances for the rays of the sun to permeate the dark, damp shroud of cover. Some town folks say nature is playing a hand in carpeting its exterior in greenery to keep the many secrets within its walls while the ghost of old man Ramsey walks the halls.

It remains on the tour list of mansions and plantations to be visited in the tidewater area of Virginia. Tourists enjoy hearing the fascinating stories of the aristocratic Ramsey family and fantasize vicariously living in great opulence, which many years ago included extravagant balls, exciting hunting parties and visits by European royalty.

There had been a few Ramsey men throughout generations who did not rise to the high moral and social standards expected, but the mischievous pranks of those few mavericks were greatly overshadowed by the generous deeds of other family members, and the Ramseys enjoyed a reputation for their benevolence. Many charities in York County, and in fact the state, had been established by the Ramsey women. Some people in the county greatly admired the Ramseys and protected the character of the name to all outsiders.

These people felt a strong bond of loyalty to the Ramsey family and believed that if it had not been for them, many of their progenitors would not have survived. Over the generations, there had been great depressions when many of the county residents lost everything and turned to the Ramsey family for assistance. The Ramseys always came through with support and provided a living existence for them in their time of need.

It was true, though, that much of the plantation's six thousand acres was confiscated from poor, indigent neighbors during the depression years. Some felt there were shady foreclosure deals where the banks closed their eyes, and the Ramseys were waiting and eager to add the property to their already extensive landholdings. Some people felt the foreclosures were acted upon too hastily, but others felt the Ramseys were acting in good faith to help out in an already bad financial situation. For this reason, it was a little easier for some folks in York County to overlook certain indiscretions of the Ramsey family.

For generations, the Ramsey name was synonymous with money and power. The six thousand acres of rich farmland yielded copious crops of tobacco. Over the years, family interests expanded from the tobacco fields and diversified into the banking industry and the commodities market. Money came as easily to the Ramseys as leaves falling from a tree.

BillyJoe Coleman was the caretaker, as had been his grandfather before him. In fact, the Coleman family could trace its heritage back eighty-seven years as being the plantation's caretakers. There were no Ramseys to tend the plantation, now. The property had been tied up in probate after the matriarch of the plantation, Patricia Ramsey, died—and that was over twelve years ago.

Patricia, or Miss Patti as she was fondly called, was the last of the Ramseys, or so it was presumed. It was said she died of a broken heart. She lived a long life—too long for the misery and heartache she had sustained. Years of dreadful events took their toll. Her carefree, ebullient personality turned into a rather dark, contemplative mood at times after her husband lost his life in a tragic hunting accident. Those close to her always felt her mood swings had something to do with her son, Henry.

Henry was an exceptionally good looking young man...tall, with an athletic physique, a quick, mischievous smile and vibrant blue eyes. He was a spitting image of his father, but he lacked his charm and charisma. He was an only child and greatly over indulged to an extent that he was spoiled beyond belief. He loved to flaunt his family power and money over the other boys in the area...especially the plantation caretaker's son, BillyJoe. Henry (or Hank as his friends called him) was the town bully. His father had bailed him out of trouble with the sheriff's office more than once.

When he grew to manhood, he showed no real ambition and wanted no responsibility in overseeing the needs of the plantation. Tobacco fields, banking interests and the commodities market held no interest for him. In his youth, he was looked upon as one of the

Ramsey mavericks and so his actions were excused. It was quite different, however, when he returned from college, as his pranks were no longer cute. They became much more serious in nature and often times were too dangerous.

Two years after old man Ramsey's accidental death, Henry was killed, but family ties had long been broken between mother and son. All communication between the two ended about the time old man Ramsey was accidentally killed while fox hunting with a group of friends. Miss Patti never spoke to her son after the accident, nor were any of the servants allowed to speak his name in her presence. She gave no reason, and none was expected. Miss Patti was loved by all and her wishes were greatly respected. It was said she did lament not knowing Henry's wife, Alice, more intimately, for supposedly Alice died while giving birth to a baby girl seven months after Henry had been killed. No one knew that for certain. If it were true, the baby would be Miss Patti's only grandchild and would be in line to inherit the plantation. Alice disappeared shortly after Henry's funeral and never made contact with Miss Patti.

Over the years, BillyJoe had hired several detectives to find out if Henry's wife, Alice, did indeed give birth to a daughter. If there were a daughter born to Alice Ramsey, she would be the sole heir to the plantation. No matter, which detective agency BillyJoe hired, he always received the same telegram report: "Hospital records verify there was a daughter Rachel born to a Mrs. Henry (Alice) Ramsey. Death report filed at time of birth for Alice. Trail leads to daughter Rachel in Paris where all leads end." BillyJoe felt a great obligation to the memory of Miss Patti to locate her granddaughter and he remained persistent in his continuing search to find her. It was this long search for Rachel that delayed action in the probate court.

*****

Seth Coleman lived with his dad, BillyJoe, on the plantation. When he was a small boy, the mansion was a hiding place where he could retreat after being scolded by his father. Scoldings weren't too often as he remembered; more in the summertime when the tourists visited the mansion. Now, at twenty-two, Seth realized there was a pattern to the time of the scoldings—either after his dad had been drinking or after he had shown the tourists around the mansion and the plantation.

Jeannine Dahlberg

Seth felt he needed a break between the academic rigors of college and entering the competitive business world. Graduation from Washington University in St. Louis from the School of Architecture fulfilled his dream of becoming an architect, but he wanted a few months of free time for himself before joining the architectural firm of Joseph A. Gabriel and Son in Wilmington.

He had always been fascinated with the idea that he could locate Alice Ramsey's daughter. Growing up on the Ramsey plantation and playing in the antebellum mansion fostered within him a tight web of emotions linking the two families—the Ramseys, landlords; and the Colemans, caretakers. He believed the detective agencies did not have the personal interest and perseverance to pursue the investigation, aborting their search too soon. The trip abroad would provide the much needed relaxation time and would justify his romping around Europe over the summer. Besides, it would afford him the opportunity to be an inscrutable investigator like his mystery hero, Charlie Chan. He decided to approach his dad with the idea of traveling to Paris during the summer to see if he could pick up the trail to find Rachel.

CHAPTER TWO

"Do you have all of the investigative reports in your briefcase, son?" BillyJoe asked. "You know, it's not going to be easy tracking a trail that's cold and years old."

"Dad, that's going to be the fun and challenge of the whole investigation. I plan to pick up where the detectives left off, at the St. Jeanne d'Arc Hospital in Paris." Seth countered.

The good-byes at the airport were brief. BillyJoe was pensive with his thoughts of his son embarking on a search that may lead to unraveling the mystery of the disappearance of Alice Ramsey. His ambiguous feelings of finding Rachel belied the fact that BillyJoe knew more about Alice's disappearance than he was willing to divulge to his son.

Seth was excited with the idea of probing for information about Alice and her daughter, Rachel. He studied all the investigative reports on the plane to Paris, giving close attention to every detail outlined by the detectives. All agencies agreed: Alice Ramsey died at childbirth at the St. Jeanne d'Arc Hospital in Paris in April 1930. A daughter, Rachel, was born and taken to Orleans Orphanage where she was put up for adoption. The detectives reported the trail had ended at the orphanage because it had been destroyed during the war.

Seth reflected upon the many mystery novels he had read and the investigative prowess of Charlie Chan. He found himself daydreaming and became a little disconcerted when the plane rolled onto the tarmac in Paris. As he stepped off the plane, he had the feeling his trip to Europe would be a real adventure and he was eager to get started.

*****

Seth's room lacked the ambiance of a first-class hotel, but it was sufficient for his needs. His one window did provide a nice view of a small portion of Paris and he marveled at its beauty. The citizens had saved their beautiful city from the ravages of World War II by surrendering to the Germans early in the War. He could see the Notre Dame Cathedral from his window and tried to remember his history and world geography classes and the role this church played in the evolution of history. He soon forgot those thoughts and concentrated on the architectural design with the flying buttresses and high steeple spires, which seemed to touch the sky. His attention turned to his desire to design beautiful buildings that would withstand the test of time. He was by nature a dreamer and could be lost in his own creative world for minutes on end. Perhaps, some day, he would design a church that would be as structurally important to architecture as Notre Dame, and this would be his legacy to the world. With these thoughts, he fell asleep.

The morning sun shone through the crack in the shutters at the window and cast a stream of light onto Seth's bed. A pesky fly, which had found its way through the unscreened window circled over his head, and Seth decided it was time to get up. He dressed quickly and bounced down the stairs (the elevator was not working) to ask the hotel manager directions to St. Jeanne d'Arc Hospital.

The hotel manager was very accommodating and spoke fluent English with absolutely no French accent, which surprised Seth. After a quick breakfast at one of the many sidewalk cafes, he hailed a taxi to go to St. Jeanne d'Arc Hospital.

The sisters at the hospital were not as accommodating as the hotel manager and treated Seth rather snobbishly. He was told that records for Alice Ramsey were marked confidential and they could say no more than Alice Ramsey had died at childbirth and a daughter was taken to Orleans Orphanage for adoption. Seth sat all day in the foyer of the hospital hoping to catch someone who would divulge a little bit more information. His smiles and cheerfulness caught the attention of many of the younger nurses and by late afternoon he had found out that Alice Ramsey was buried in the Du Pere Lachaise cemetery. He was jubilant with this bit of information. He would be able to trace the burial records to the person or persons who paid for interment. He decided it was a good day's work and walked back to the hotel.

The hotel manager was at the desk.

"You sure do speak good English for being a Frenchman," Seth jovially said as he walked up to the desk.

"Who's a Frenchman? I was born in the good ol' U.S. of A. Hi, my name's John Gravin and I'm from Davenport, Iowa," the hotel manager retorted.

"Well, it is a small world. What are you doing working behind the desk?" Seth questioned.

Riding the Tail of the Dragon

The conversation with John proved to be quite informative. John was an American GI, who served under General Patton during the War. He decided to stay in France after the War to help the French recover from the devastation. It was during the course of this conversation that John mentioned rebuilding an orphanage that had been destroyed by the French Resistance. At the time, the building had been taken over by the Nazis to be used as an armory and all the children had been moved to another location. By coincidence, it was the Orleans Orphanage that John was talking about, and Seth wondered what the odds were to find someone in all of Paris who would remember and know the circumstances of the Orleans Orphanage being destroyed. He felt it was just dumb luck. It was turning out to be a great day.

The evening was as pleasant as the day had been. John invited him to dinner at his home where he met the real reason for John's staying in Paris after the War. John literally beamed with pride when he introduced Seth to his wife, Diedre. It was quite evident it was a good marriage. Diedre was a beautiful French woman with the artistic ability of being a superb cook. Seth tried not to devour the meal so quickly as he had become accustomed while keeping up with the other boys in the frat house and the rapid pace of college life. The dinner wine seemed to bother him more than usual, however, which he attributed to lack of sleep. He was still trying to overcome the difference in time and the sleep he lost in traveling abroad. The excitement of the day had kept his adrenaline going and he forgot all about how tired he was, but now the effects of the wine were starting to play havoc with his sensibility. He bade the Gravins good night and retired early, anticipating another great day.

John had mentioned the night before that the Du Pere Lachaise cemetery was within walking distance of the hotel. It was a long walk, but Seth thought it best to conserve his money as he wasn't certain how long he would be in Paris.

As he strolled the cemetery grounds, reading the names on the tombstones, he started daydreaming of the past lives of these people. The cemetery was very old…with famous people such as Chopin, Bizet, Oscar Wilde and many more buried there. He found himself being caught up in an atmosphere, which enveloped him mentally into an earlier time in history, where struggles for life, beauty and knowledge were the same as they were in the Deep South before the Civil War.

These thoughts made him reflect upon life as it must have been on the Ramsey plantation at this period of time. The stories told by his grandfather were quite vivid in his memory and definitely made an impression upon a young boy.

The cemetery was quite large and Seth hoped he could find someone who could direct him to the records office. He found a caretaker with whom it was quite difficult to converse, but learned the records office was located at the far end of the cemetery. At this point, Seth wished he would have paid closer attention in class when he studied French. He was quickly finding out many Frenchmen did not like to converse in any language other than their own and he certainly wasn't fluent in French.

He entered the small, musky smelling office and approached the woman in attendance. He asked to see the interment records for April 1930. The book was very old and rather large. Upon opening it, he discovered the entries were clearly and legibly written. The thrill and excitement he felt in finding the information was soon shattered as he read the name BillyJoe Coleman, York County, Virginia, on the line indicating the next of kin responsible for payment of the interment of Alice Ramsey.

Seth couldn't believe what he was reading and fixed his eyes sharply on the page. He read the line over and over again, hoping the name would change. What did this mean? Why hadn't his dad told him he knew where Alice Ramsey was buried? And, next of kin? What did that mean? The Colemans were certainly not the next of kin to the Ramseys. Seth closed the interment ledger in a daze of disbelief and returned it to the attendant. He wandered aimlessly on the paths of the cemetery to the exit and no longer read the names inscribed on the tombstones, as he was now deep in his own troubled thoughts.

The long walk back to the hotel provided ample time to consider his next plan of action. He would have to place a collect call to his dad, expensive or not. He had to know why his dad kept this important information from him.

Riding the Tail of the Dragon

As he pushed the revolving door into the hotel lobby, he called out to John, "What would it take for you to place a call to my dad in Virginia?"

"A lot of time and a lot of money. Let me see what I can do," John replied.

Seth waited for over an hour in the lobby while John pursued the central phone operator to place the collect call to the States. Finally, the phone rang, and Seth eagerly grabbed the receiver.

"Dad, what's going on?" Seth blurted. "There are a lot of questions I want to have answered. I've uncovered a bit of information that is more than disconcerting, it's downright baffling and I don't understand it." The tone of his voice was high pitched and anxious, and BillyJoe knew he had found a piece of information that he didn't want discovered.

"Now, son, take it easy. Don't get so excited. What is it that you want to know?" BillyJoe said in as calm a voice as he could muster.

"Well, for starters, why is your name on the interment record book as paying for the burial of Alice Ramsey? Why are you listed as next to kin? Why didn't you tell the detective agencies about this, and why in the heck didn't you tell me?" Seth blurted out in one breath and still in a high-pitched voice.

"That's a whole lot of information you want to know on this long-distance call, son. Why don't you just continue your search for Rachel and I will answer all your questions when you come home." BillyJoe tried to make his voice sound soothing and in control.

"I hope you're not holding anything else back from me, dad. It's difficult enough trying to converse with these Frenchmen, let alone being shocked by a bit of information discovered at the cemetery. I'll continue my search, but I hope there are no more surprises." Seth countered.

"Okay, son. We'd better end this call while I can still pay for it." BillyJoe said jokingly and bid his son goodnight. He placed the phone on the cradle, looked out the window across the field to the Ramsey mansion, and grabbed the bottle of bourbon from the kitchen cabinet. He hoped he was doing the right thing by trying to locate Rachel Ramsey.

BillyJoe sat at the kitchen table for a long time drinking one shot of bourbon after another trying to obliterate any remembrances of his

Jeannine Dahlberg

childhood, but to no avail. Flashes of dark, irritating memories sparked thoughts of an unpleasant youth endured in the shadow of Hank Ramsey.

As young boys growing up on the plantation, both were the same age, but that's where the similarity stopped. Hank was the priviledged one, being the only son of a wealthy plantation owner. And Henry Ramsey, Sr. made it quite clear to BillyJoe that he was to look after Hank and try to keep him out of trouble. That became a monumental task for BillyJoe and there were many times when he wished he hadn't been born.

BillyJoe's mother, Vickie Lee, probably wished the same thing many times as she abandoned BillyJoe when he was two years old. A young bride at sixteen and a mother at seventeen, Vickie Lee cried herself to sleep many nights rationalizing there was more to life than washing diapers. She wanted to feel young and free and yearned for the excitement of New Orleans. The many magazines, which covered the kitchen table, colorfully illustrated life on Bourbon Street with its speakeasies, dixieland bands and raucous parties. At nineteen, she felt cloistered and unhappy with a sense of pity that life was passing her by. The last time BillyJoe heard from his mother she was living in New Orleans and was trying to make it big as a singer.

Miss Patti insisted BillyJoe live in the mansion so he could be a playmate for Hank. This arrangement worked very well for a few years. But as personalities and attitudes developed in the young boys, Hank became extremely difficult to control. Too often, BillyJoe had to lie to the sheriff to protect Hank.

BillyJoe gulped another shot of burbon. The room was starting to spin and he rested his head on the table. Memories of Hank's wicked pranks loomed before him, enlarged and distorted by the affects of alcohol. There was no mistake, however, that Hank would have drowned a classmate at the school picnic if he had not interceded and pulled Hank off the boy.

BillyJoe raised his head from the table and cupped his hands over his ears to stifle the sound of Hank's laughter. If he could only push that sound out of his head forever. With each evil prank, Hank's cacophonous laughter became more shrill. Somehow, he would have to forget the past, even if it meant pouring it from a bottle. With this thought, he fell asleep.

*****

Seth sat quietly in the hotel lobby for awhile after his phone conversation. He needed time to digest the short dialogue he had with his dad, which divulged no information. His exuberance and excitement at finding Rachel ebbed and his ambivalent feelings gave way to pensive thoughts.

As he walked by the lobby desk, he noticed John was busy talking to hotel guests. He felt a little relieved as he was in no mood for trivial chatter and he slowly ascended the stairs to his room.

He pondered the events of the day. The information uncovered at the cemetery was absolutely of no value to him in locating Rachel. To his bewilderment, his dad was the missing link in the disappearance of Alice, but he did not know what had happened to Rachel.

His enthusiasm and eagerness to find Rachel was, as Seth realized, a ploy to "play at" being a detective like Charlie Chan and at the same time have a little bit of summer fun. With the discovery involving his dad in the disappearance of Alice Ramsey, the investigation was becoming much more serious in nature and it made him feel uneasy. Perhaps he would uncover something he really didn't want to know. He wished his dad would have answered his questions over the phone, as he would have felt better about continuing the search for Rachel.

He rationalized the only reason to discover the whereabouts of Rachel was so she could inherit the Ramsey plantation. After all, his dad had been trying to find her for over eighteen years. There was probably a simple explanation why his dad's name was on the interment records at the cemetery for Alice. He would let it suffice he would have the answers to his questions when he returned home.

When Seth put his head on the pillow that night, it had not been a good day. He wondered what lay ahead tomorrow.

Jeannine Dahlberg

CHAPTER THREE

"Good morning, Diedre. I didn't know you work at the hotel, too?" Seth asked brightly as he entered the lobby.

"Well, not on a regular basis, thank goodness. Occasionally, John likes to work in the construction business with a few of his old friends. He says physical work is good exercise, but I really think he prefers working outdoors rather than being cooped up in this hotel." Diedre said. "And where are you off to this morning?"

"John mentioned the other evening he helped to rebuild the Orleans Orphanage after the War, and I was hoping he could tell me how to get there. I don't know my way around Paris very well, yet, and I was hoping he could point me in the right direction."

Diedre looked at Seth rather quizzically. "I must have been in the kitchen cooking when you and John discussed the orphanage. Why do you want to go to the fashion bureau? Are you a designer?"

Seth didn't understand the question. He asked, "What do you mean am I a designer? I'm looking for the Orleans Orphanage."

"There is no Orleans Orphanage. That building was destroyed during the War. John worked on constructing another building on the same site, which is called The House of Design where many of France's dress designers have their studios. The orphanage, that is the children were moved to a location outside Paris during the War and I suppose that's what you're looking for, am I right?"

Diedre wondered why a young man would be interested in finding an orphanage. Certainly he wasn't considering adopting a child. He wasn't married. She believed him to be one of the most handsome young men she had seen in a long time (barring her husband)...tall, broad shouldered, with a winning smile and gentle personality. He could surely melt any girl's heart and she wondered if he had a girl back home.

"Yeah, Diedre, that's right," Seth answered. "I want to know where the orphanage relocated so I can try to find a girl who was placed in the home shortly after birth, and it's imperative that I find her as quickly as possible. Of course, she would be much older now."

"This girl, is she related to you?" Diedre asked.

"No, but it's extremely important that I find her. She is the sole heir to inherit a large plantation in Virginia, and my dad, who is the caretaker for the plantation, told the Virginia courts he would try to find her," Seth explained. "I volunteered to do some investigating myself, since I have some free time this summer before starting work in the fall, and I thought it would be fun to bum around Europe for a few months. The detective agents my dad hired were unable to locate the orphanage. They didn't have the stroke of luck that I have had in meeting you and John."

Seth stared out the lobby window and wondered what the odds are in finding someone in Paris so quickly who remembers where the Orleans' orphans were taken. He turned to Diedre and asked, "How far outside Paris is the orphanage? Could you direct me, or perhaps draw a map for me so I won't get lost?"

"Oh, I can do better than that," Diedre smiled. "I'll ask my little stepsister, Sarah, to take you there. She likes to read stories to the children on Sunday afternoons. I'll get in touch with her and let you know tonight if she will be free tomorrow."

Diedre resumed her work at the desk and shook her head in disbelief at the stack of paperwork that was before her. She wondered if John ever kept the hotel records up to date.

Seth relished the idea of having a free day to see some of the sights of Paris. The view of the Seine River and the city from atop the Eiffel Tower was breathtaking. He could also make out France's miniature statue, which is a replica of the Statue of Liberty in New York harbor. He remembered from one of his history classes that the Statue of Liberty was given to the United States by the French government. It reminded him of home and his dad. His mind immediately focused on his dad's intimate connection to Alice Ramsey. Thoughts seemed to ramble around in his head growing more bizarre in substance until he stopped cold with the salacious thought that his dad and Alice had been lovers. Could it be that Rachel was his dad's and Alice's daughter? Maybe that was the real reason for locating Rachel. That would mean Rachel would be his half-sister. There were so many questions to be answered.

The day was long and hot. Paris was starting to lose its charm in the heat as he meandered the walkway along the river. He enjoyed looking over the shoulders of the many artists who were positioned along the river capturing an alluring view onto their canvases. He admired their creative talent and hoped some day he could be able to design beautiful buildings that would be admired by others.

As he sat on the bank of the River Seine with his back against a tree, a soft breeze whispered past, which carried his thoughts into a dream world. He was a romantic who enjoyed conjuring up daydreams of mystical vignettes that were pleasing to his intellectual liking. The hours passed with little concern for the impending investigation and the afternoon melted away into evening before he returned to the hotel.

Diedre had left a message at the desk that Sarah would be able to meet him at nine o'clock in the morning in the hotel lobby to take him to the orphanage. Seth was happy with the thought of having someone with him who would be fluent in French. He was eager to get started and looked forward to picking up Rachel's trail. He had concerns about soliciting the adoption records and wondered how Charlie Chan would proceed.

CHAPTER FOUR

The cheerful chirping of a robin on his windowsill awoke Seth at daybreak, and he lay in bed another two hours before showering and dressing. Sleep did not return as his mind was racing with thoughts of the impending trip to the orphanage. When he entered the lobby to await the arrival of Sarah, he had already been awake over four hours and his energy level definitely needed some reinforcement of a hearty breakfast. Diedre was again at the front desk and bid good morning to Seth. She volunteered the name of a restaurant around the corner from the hotel that served good egg omelets and sausage at an inexpensive price and said she would send Sarah there to meet him.

Seth's appetite was more than satisfied and he marveled at how much better he felt after eating breakfast. He enjoyed the quiet time at his small table next to a window and noticed the streets of Paris were starting to become alive with pedestrians. He liked to watch people and played a game where he would imagine the lifestyles and occupations of the pedestrians passing by the cafe.

A quick glance at his watch revealed it was almost ten o'clock. He started to fidget with the salt shaker on the table and looked anxiously out the window for Sarah.

At a distance down the street, he noticed a girl about sixteen years old walking briskly toward the restaurant. Her long dark auburn hair bounced on her shoulders. Her skirt and blouse were typically American, including the bobby socks and black and white saddle shoes. As she came closer, Seth knew this young girl was Diedre's stepsister, Sarah. Her resemblance to Diedre was striking, but she looked so "Americanized". Seth stood to meet Sarah and introduced himself.

"Hi. I'm Seth. You must be Sarah."

"Yeah. Sorry I'm late, but I had to wait for Larry to return to the taxi stand. He's going to take us to the orphanage. It's quite a distance outside Paris. Hope you didn't mind waiting a little."

Seth noticed her eyes seemed to dance as she talked. She bubbled with enthusiasm.

"Come on, Seth, we had better hurry before Larry picks up another fare. He said he would wait only a few minutes, and he hates to wait for anyone."

Upon meeting Larry, it was quite evident he was infatuated with Sarah. His eyes never left her.

The conversation during the drive to the orphanage was quite pleasant. This was his first opportunity to enjoy talking with people close to his own age since he had arrived in Paris. Larry was a struggling student trying to earn money so he could continue his education in political science. The War was still a bitter memory, but he was determined to use the experience to his benefit in serving France in the diplomatic corps. When he spoke of his personal life, he glanced many times at Sarah until Seth thought the taxi would run off the road. Sarah blushed with embarrassment and changed the subject.

Sarah talked happily about the youngsters in the orphanage. Every weekend she would visit and read or tell stories to the smaller children. She felt this was her contribution to the rehabilitation of Paris. Many children were the offsprings of an illegitimate union between a French woman and a soldier of the occupying army.

Seth asked Sarah if she knew where the administration offices were so they could locate the files for children accepted into the orphanage in 1930. Sarah explained at great length how she had volunteered to work in the orphanage over the past two years and had assisted in all departments of administration before realizing her talent lay in telling children stories. Her fresh approach and youthful ideas in relating stories, which appealed to the children were recognized by the Sisters of the orphanage to be inspired by God. Sarah didn't disagree with this assumption, but felt a little uncomfortable and embarrassed when the Sisters poured their admiration and satisfaction upon her.

She told Seth some files were locked in a safe, which she determined were for security reasons and no one but the Mother Superior was allowed to look at those files.

A sick thought flashed through Seth's mind that perhaps Rachel's file may be in that safe. He hoped not.

The taxi followed a narrow road through countryside that was absolutely beautiful with verdant rolling hills, hedgerows and a vast

Riding the Tail of the Dragon

forest. It was easy to understand why the children were moved to this area. It was an ideal, secluded location for an orphanage. It had been a safe haven for small children trying to survive the ravages of war. Seth could visualize a frantic scene where frightened children were quickly hustled out of Paris during the early days of the War to this retreat. He figured there were probably hundreds of both happy and tragic stories that could be told about the orphans who were brought here, which thought made him most anxious to see the files.

Larry pulled the taxi to a stop at the front gates of the drive and asked the gatekeeper for permission to enter. The gatekeeper was ready to give Larry a hard time when he noticed Sarah in the back seat and quickly motioned them forward.

Seth and Sarah waived good-bye to Larry and quickly walked up the steps to the front door and into the grand entrance hall. It was almost lunch time and the hallways emanating from the entrance hall were crowded with children heading for the dining room. When the children saw Sarah, they swarmed around her as if she were the Pied Piper. Hugs and kisses were exchanged as Sarah pushed her way down the hallway toward a sign that read, "Administration Office". Seth was a few paces behind trying not to stumble over the smaller children.

The receptionist was a jovial, heavyset woman. She gave a quick smile to Sarah and asked if the young man with her was going to entertain the children. Sarah told her of his desire to locate a girl who had been taken into the orphanage in 1930 and asked for permission to view the files from that year.

The receptionist gave Seth a quizzical look and hesitated for a moment. Sarah quickly enforced the urgency of the request by weaving a story of her own, which totally baffled Seth. She was indeed a good storyteller. The receptionist obliged and brought the files to the counter where Sarah and Seth poured over them for an hour.

To their great disappointment, they could not find any records of the admission of Rachel Ramsey. Seth's dreaded fear was now a reality. Rachel's files must be locked in the safe. Sarah agreed.

The files were returned to the receptionist and they decided they would have to ask the Mother Superior for the secured files.

Jeannine Dahlberg

On the surface, it seemed like such a simple request. Both were talking at the same time as they strolled down the hallway to Mother Superior's office. They knew they had to deliver a convincing story to Mother Superior in order to invade the privacy of records that had been held for so many years under lock and key.

Both agreed Seth would tell the story; Sarah would translate it into French and then she would make the request for the records. After all, she was Mother Superior's favorite volunteer worker at the orphanage. Sarah knocked on the door and was bade to enter.

Seth couldn't explain his emotions as he entered the room. He was extremely nervous, almost to the point of visibly shaking. He again wished his knowledge of the French language were a whole lot better as he would feel more comfortable speaking directly to the Mother Superior. He gave himself a quick pep talk and remembered that he had survived being a pledge in the fraternity house; he had suffered through long hours of study for college exams; and he had won the dare when he was eight years old to spend a night alone in the Ramsey mansion where it was rumored ghosts walked the halls. He took a deep breath and tried to regain his composure. After Sarah introduced Seth to the Mother Superior, they were asked to sit down in front of a beautifully hand-carved desk.

Seth studied furniture design in his sophomore year of college and, if memory served him right, the carving on the front panel of the desk resembled workmanship from the Napoleonic era. Seeking to ease the tense atmosphere, Seth asked Sarah to inquire if Napoleon's brother had designed it. Mother Superior, realizing that Seth did not speak French, graciously added that she would be more than happy to speak in English as she seldom got the opportunity. Sarah was as surprised as Seth that the Mother Superior could speak English, but relished the thought of not having to translate everything.

Mother Superior spoke at great length, in American English dialect as opposed to British English, explaining how the orphanage acquired the desk. She definitely considered it to be a treasure and was quite pleased that a young man should know about design and craftsmanship. Seth began to relax a little with his nervous tension ebbing. He was anxious to find out how the Mother Superior learned to speak English so well, but he decided to ask that question later.

Riding the Tail of the Dragon

Mother Superior's voice seemed to fade in the distance as the thought of obtaining the files enveloped Seth's concentration to the point that he did not hear Mother Superior's question of why the unexpected visit from Sarah and her friend.

Sarah nudged Seth with her elbow, for she, too, wanted to know why Seth was searching for a young woman who had been given up at birth to an orphanage so many years ago.

Seth felt the stares of both Sarah and the Mother Superior and quickly raised his head to respond. Thoughts seemed to race through his mind. Should he weave a story of intrigue that, hopefully, would unlock the files or should he tell a story that would be the truth as he knew it. A minute elapsed before he started to answer, but it seemed more like a lifetime. He decided upon honesty and told the story with alacrity.

He could hear his father's words in the back of his brain and the story seemed to unfold as if his father were talking about the Ramsey plantation. At times he faltered when speaking of the Ramsey son, Henry. It was always when speaking of Henry that his father's words were said quite vehemently. Seth did not fully understand why, but repeated the words in the same tone of voice. He told of the detectives who were hired to locate Alice in Paris and their discovery that a baby girl, Rachel, had been born to Alice at the St. Jeanne d'Arc Hospital in 1930. He told of Patricia Ramsey's death and the possibility of Rachel being the sole heir to inherit the Ramsey plantation. He squirmed in his chair and became visibly nervous. He hesitated a moment in telling the story and then divulged that his father and Alice Ramsey had a brief relationship, which resulted in Alice's becoming pregnant. His voice became low, filled with emotion and then inaudible. He cleared his throat more than once in order to continue the story. To Seth, it seemed quite logical. That would explain why his father's name was on the interment records for Alice Ramsey and he continued to rationalize that his father wanted to find his daughter. Seth decided to embellish upon this part of the story so as to appeal to Mother Superior's emotions and repeated the urgent need to locate Rachel. Tears welled in his eyes and his voice wavered to speak the words, "I would like to meet my half-sister."

Jeannine Dahlberg

The office remained quiet for several minutes as each reflected upon the story. It was Sarah who broke the silence to ask the Mother Superior if she would allow Seth to review the secured files.

The Mother Superior looked curiously, but tenderly, over the rim of her glasses at the two young figures, contemplating the issue at hand. The confidentiality of certain files had never been violated since the end of the War. They were, in fact, secured files.

Mother Superior stood and walked to the window. The room was quiet and Seth knew everyone could hear his heart beating.

"Do you know for a fact the baby was named Rachel? And, what proof do you have that Alice Ramsey was the mother?" she asked.

Seth removed the hospital report from his jacket and handed it to the Mother Superior.

As she sat down at the desk, she held her head in her hands—almost in disbelief at the name on the report. Of all the little children who had lived at the orphanage, Rachel Ramsey was a name she would never forget. A rush of years past conjured up memories of hardships endured during the War. They were bitter years when the Germans occupied France. She recalled a parade of officers who visited the orphanage, but there was one general whose name she would always remember—Erik von Horsemann.

"There is no need to retrieve the files, for I know the circumstances quite well," she sighed. She placed her head on the back of the chair, closed her eyes as if to relive those years and proceeded to tell the story.

"As you have found out, the orphanage was located in Paris and was known as the Orleans Orphanage. My goodness, I was quite young, as I guess we all were. I was not privileged to be the Mother Superior then, but helped with the young children and babies who were orphaned for one reason or another.

"Rachel was brought to us when she was only days old. We were told she was American with no known relatives in France. She was a beautiful baby and all the Sisters fell in love with her immediately. She had such a pleasant disposition, blond hair and blue eyes and seldom cried.

"Early in the War when the Nazis occupied Paris, it was quite common for the German officers to bring their illegitimate offsprings to us; that was the reason for maintaining secured files.

Riding the Tail of the Dragon

"But in Rachel's case, it was quite different. General Erik von Horstmann's wife had lost a baby girl while giving birth and she was devastated to the point of being suicidal. The general and his wife were vacationing in Paris at the time and the general came to us and asked if we had a baby girl he could adopt.

"Of course, the general never conveyed his reason for seeking to adopt a child from an orphanage in France, but I suppose it had something to do with Hitler's rising to power at that time, and the general didn't want the German high command to know that he planned to adopt a child.

"When he first saw Rachel, he knew that she would be the little girl his wife could love.

"It was years later, in the spring of 1941, when the general's name appeared in the paper. He was in North Africa with Field Marshal Rommel and the 7th Panzer Division. As I recall, the article was very flattering to both Rommel and von Horstmann, as their being among Germany's greatest military strategists.

"Thereafter, I read the paper with more care, as I was quite interested in following General von Horstmann's brilliant military career. I suppose I felt a concern for his safety even though he was a German. Meeting him personally at the orphanage and watching baby Rachel Ramsey cuddle in his strong arms at the time of the adoption created within me a vicarious feeling of motherhood. He had adopted a baby girl who had found her way into my heart. When the general left the orphanage that afternoon with Rachel, I cried for a part of me went with him."

There was a long pause. Seth and Sarah sat motionless as they both looked at the Mother Superior. Her eyes were still closed. She remained silent not wanting to break the spell that enveloped her. It was evident that her love for Rachel had extended the bounds of the Sister's care of the orphaned children.

Neither Seth nor Sarah wanted to ask questions at this point. They respected Mother Superior's mood and waited for her to regain her composure. Her head fell forward from the back of the chair and her eyes opened. Tears rimmed her eyes as she continued.

"The general's name appeared many times in the paper—most often in articles regarding Rommel. It was after the second battle of el-Alamein when Rommel's Panzers were defeated that General von

Horstmann and Field Marshall Rommel were ordered by Hitler to return to Germany. The War was now going very poorly for the Germans. The general's name appeared in the paper many months later when he was ordered to assist Rommel in setting up defenses along our coast. The coast of France would again be in jeopardy of heavy fighting.

"Oh, those were painful, distressing days. By day, we feared we would not have enough food for the children nor enough fuel to keep them warm; and by night, we listened to the yells of our people being dragged from their homes by the Gestapo. They were superb craftsmen of War. Sometimes, it was no more than a tactical exercise.

"It was rumored they wanted our orphanage for a garrison post, and we felt it was just a matter of time before we would be forced to leave. Where would we go? Our children; our poor children. In secret, we held mass, praying the Americans and the Brits would liberate us and return Paris to the French people again.

"In our small way, we helped the French Resistance occasionally by hiding someone in the orphanage. We knew it was a dangerous thing to do, but everyone of us, the Sisters and the older children, decided we wanted to help fight the Germans. They were becoming more brutal as the War dragged from one perilous day to another. It was amazing the bonding, loyalty and camaraderie we felt for one another. We were a big family, now. United by a desperate cause to sustain life. I believe it was the adrenaline that flowed through our veins stimulating our bodies and minds that made us brave.

"It was early spring in 1944 when an old car pulled in front of the orphanage. We, of course, were suspicious of anyone stopping by the orphanage. Three people got out: a man and woman dressed as farmers and a young girl. We were even more surprised to learn that the man was General Erik von Horstmann with his wife and daughter. And we were elated when we realized the young girl was Rachel. What a beautiful child; quite a little lady. I was thrilled to see the love the general and Frau Horstmann expressed for Rachel. She, of course, didn't remember the orphanage or me. It was astounding how visiting with one of our charges for just a few hours brought such happiness to the Sisters. We were able to forget for a short time the dreadful, fearful existence we were experiencing under the German occupation.

"The general quickly hustled us all into the anteroom, and with a sense of urgency explained their deceptive dress. We were shocked to learn he wanted Frau Horstmann and Rachel to stay with us at the orphanage."

Mother Superior fixed her gaze on Sarah and Seth and said, "If you two can imagine how we felt. His request was like an electrical charge that went around the room. My body stiffened with fear and I thought my chest would cave in with a sinking heart. Why would a high-ranking German officer make such an extraordinary request of a poor, little orphanage? The pleasure we felt at seeing Rachel swiftly vanished. We were now suspicious of their visit. Our first inclination was to think it was a ploy to uncover our participation with the French Resistance.

"The mood changed so quickly that the general was forced to divulge his own secret. He took a bible from the table and held it in his hand. Then he asked every one of us to join hands with him, forming a long chain, and to swear we would never disclose the identities of Frau Horstmann and Rachel. He proceeded to tell his story."

Seth sat riveted in his chair under the stare of the Mother Superior. Her eyes were focused upon him, but they were windows into the frightening past. Her compelling gaze substantiated the horrific plot that was to unfold.

Mother Superior spoke in a low voice—almost a whisper as if she were afraid after all these years that someone would enter the room and hear the story.

"The general warned that he had intercepted a message from Berlin disclosing the orphanage was suspect of aiding the Resistance. It was this classified information that prompted him to seek our help. He told us he had responded to the message to Berlin's satisfaction that he would personally investigate all charges and would keep them advised.

"He explained it was necessary for the identities of Frau Horstmann and Rachel to be concealed. I could see he was wrestling with his thoughts, trying to decide if he should explain in more detail. He looked around the room at all of us as we stood petrified, still holding hands. He confided there were several ill-fated plots to assassinate Hitler that had gone sour and that all high-ranking officers were suspects. Taking extreme precautions, he had managed to get Frau Horstmann and Rachel out of Berlin. He now feared for his life and their lives as well. He let it suffice this was all the information we needed to know at that time.

"A week later, the general returned to the orphanage in an official capacity. As he stepped from the armored car followed by an entourage of officers, his whole countenance emitted superiority, from his beautifully tailored uniform with the red stripe running down the leg of the pants, as was worn by all German generals, to the preeminent expression on his face. Their presence instilled such fear into all of us; we trembled as we stood before them. We had taken the precaution to coach Rachel not to talk to her father if he should return unless her mother advised it was all right. The general ordered everyone to be present, including the children. This was done, of course, so he could see if Frau Horstmann and Rachel were okay. Frau Horstmann was clothed in a Sister's habit and Rachel looked like all our other little waifs, who at that time into the War were wearing tattered clothes.

"I can still remember the stern expression on his face as he glanced around the room, but I noticed the betrayal of softness in his eyes when he spotted Frau Horstmann and Rachel. Luckily, none of the accompanying officers paid any attention.

"General von Horstmann ordered the buildings to be abandoned and forcefully stated we had three days to vacate the premises. Our fears had been realized. The orphanage was to serve as command offices and quarters for the Germans in addition to the Palace at Versailles. The announcement hit me like a shot between the eyes. I quickly looked at Mother Maria Teresa, who was our Mother Superior at that time, and I thought she would faint. She had worked so hard to keep us all together. My head started to reel and my mind was racing with thoughts of where could we take the children? How could we all stay together and live?

"It was a short visit; but to us who stood trembling, it seemed like an eternity. When the general and his entourage left the grand entrance hall, I noticed there was a swagger stick on the table. I knew it was the general's because I remembered seeing pictures of him in the papers and he was always carrying one. An article, which had reported on his military career explained he was a commander of an armored tank corps, but his early military experience had been in the cavalry, and the swagger stick was in fact a riding crop.

"He alone returned to the grand hall to retrieve his riding crop and quietly and quickly explained to Mother Maria Teresa that he had selected a small villa a few miles outside of the city of Paris where he felt the children, his wife and Rachel would be safe. He wanted us to leave by the next morning, which we did. It was General von Horstmann who had been our benefactor in seeing that the orphanage received a supply of food on a regular basis. He was our savior.

"In July 1944, another plot to assassinate Hitler was unsuccessful. Hitler was paranoid to the extent that he trusted no one and suspected everyone. His bellicose personality had disintegrated to dementia. It was rumored that more than half the generals in Paris were suspected of conspiring in the stratagem. It was a terrible time for everyone. No one escaped Hitler's wrath. Beelzebub, the devil himself, could not have been more thorough and cruel in extirpating the conspirators. Field Marshall Rommel took his own life in the fall of the year for he, too, was one of the perpetrators. General von Horstmann was being sought, but managed to elude the Gestapo. Through the French underground, we found out he was hiding somewhere in France and would get word to Frau Horstmann when opportunity prevailed. Frau Horstmann anxiously awaited to hear word of his safety, as we all did."

Mother Superior again paused in telling the story, but this time Seth was not patient and interrupted her reverie.

Seth blurted out, "I don't understand. How was the general instrumental in supplying the orphanage with food."

Mother superior looked squarely at Seth as if mesmerized in a trance-like state and painfully stated, "Hitler had executed an exercise in genocide, wanting a complete annihilation of a race of people, and the general wanted no part of it. As the War progressed, the general could no longer justify these inhumane atrocities as acts of a conquering nation. After the foiled attempt in July on Hitler's life, we found out from a dear friend, Claude LaCleur, the French inspector at Interpol, that General von Horstmann had contacted him for the name of a compatriot in the French Resistance…and then the general vanished, as if swept away by the wind. Food started arriving within the week. It was always brought late at night and placed at our backdoor. In one of the first baskets of food we received was a riding crop tucked in the bottom of a bushel of potatoes. Frau Horstmann was ecstatic! Tears streamed down her cheeks; ah, those were tears of joy. She knew the riding crop was her husband's."

Sarah and Seth could hear activity in the hallway, as the children prepared to enter the dining room for dinner. The afternoon hours had quickly ebbed into evening, as the three lost all track of time. Not even the chimes from the grandfather's clock in the corner of the office had disturbed Mother Superior's soliloquy.

Mother Superior jumped to her feet as if startled by reality and said she had to leave to prepare for evening prayers.

"But Mother Superior, where is Rachel now?" Seth pleaded.

Mother Superior put her hand on Seth's arm and said, "A year or so before the war ended, General von Horstmann came for Frau Horstmann and Rachel. He said he had made arrangements to escape to South America. It was about a year later, however, when we received a short note from Rachel stating they were alive and well, but she could not tell anyone where they were. There was no return address, as the three were still in hiding. That's been quite a few years ago."

Seth, once again, felt the trail to find Rachel had ended. As he stood before Mother Superior, his thoughts played havoc with his emotions. He experienced great despair.

As he and Sarah were preparing to leave, Mother Superior said, "Wait! I still have the little note somewhere. Perhaps the postmark will be of some help to you."

She retrieved the note from a small box she kept in the lower drawer of her desk. The memorabilia looked to be years old and Seth could tell by her expression and the way she fondled the items that these were her treasures. Mother Superior looked tenderly at Seth; and as she turned over the note to him, she said, "If you find Rachel, please give her my love and blessings."

"Mother Superior, I have one more question before you go. How is it that you speak English so well...I mean, American English?" Seth asked.

"We were very fortunate to have a few American nurses stay with us immediately after the War to help us. The children's needs were great, as they had suffered from improper diet, poor clothing and insufficient medicine. Those nurses were a blessing from heaven. With exuberance and perseverance, the environment and atmosphere were lifted to new heights. We all started to laugh again and realized life was worth living. I quickly picked up English because we made a game of learning. Everyone in the orphanage learned. It turned out to be a happy time. Every evening at prayers, I give thanks to the wonderful American nurses who were dedicated to helping others."

She left the room to attend to her chores for the evening.

Both Seth and Sarah felt emotionally drained. The story, which had captivated their attention for so long, was now hard to dismiss from their thoughts. They stood quietly for a few minutes before either one moved or spoke. It was the chimes of the grandfather's clock striking five that interrupted the silence.

Sarah blurted, "Seth, look at the time! Larry was supposed to pick us up at four. Oh, I do hope he's waited. He hates it so when I run late."

They walked briskly through the halls to the front door, down the steps and onto the driveway. Larry's taxi was nowhere to be seen. Sarah hated to make Larry wait for her, as he would sound off on a tirade of the importance of promptness. She could visualize the scene. Larry would again vent his frustration, lecture her as if she were a child, and then fondly kiss her on the forehead. As they looked longingly down the road, with a feeling of abandonment and concern for a means of returning to Paris, they saw a car speeding toward them. It was Larry. The car screeched to a stop and Larry flew out the door, bursting with an apology for his being late, due to a flat tire, in a pathetic attempt to appease Sarah's anticipated anger. Sarah smiled, said nothing, and coyly nodded her acceptance of his apology.

The drive back to Paris was rather quiet. Seth's ambivalent feelings of joy that Rachel was still alive, and the dismay of not knowing where she and her parents had gone, left him speculating if he should pursue the hunt for Rachel or return to the States so he could prepare for his first professional position as an architect with

Jeannine Dahlberg

Joseph A. Gabriel and Son in Wilmington. He would have to place another call to his dad.

CHAPTER FIVE

"Well, dad, what do you think?" Seth questioned. The phone line crackled with static making the connection so poor Seth could hardly hear his dad. Seth continued, "I have found out that Inspector LaCleur is still with Interpol. I know he will be able to tell me more about General von Horstmann and where the family went after leaving Paris."

"Son, your search may have to take you to another part of the world," BillyJoe warned, "which would mean you would not be able to start your job as scheduled."

"I know, dad, but I know how important it is to you that we find Rachel, and the driving impetus to this whole search is that we find her alive." Seth urged, "I would like to continue."

"You'll need more money, son. I'll see what I can do about getting a few bucks to you as quickly as possible. Call me in a few days after you make your plans." BillyJoe said good-bye and placed the phone in its cradle. He slowly shuffled to the kitchen cabinet and pulled a bottle of whiskey from the shelf.

*****

The taxi stand wasn't too far from the hotel and Seth was hoping to catch Larry in between fares to take him to Inspector LeCleur's office at Interpol. During the drive back to Paris from the orphanage, Larry had mentioned to Seth that he would help him with transportation around Paris when he could.

"Larry," Seth called. "Could you give me a lift?"

"Sure. Where are we off to?" questioned Larry.

"I want to go to Inspector Claude LeCleur's office at Interpol. Can you spare the time to take me there?"

"Hop in, Seth. This morning is so slow. I've only had two fares. This lack of business is going to kill me. I'll never have enough money to finish courses at the university…let alone enough to ask Sarah to marry me." Larry seemed quite stressed out and talked incessantly about the fierce competition at the taxi stand, the lack of tourists in Paris and the high cost of maintaining his taxi in operational condition due to automobile tires and gasoline being scarce in all of France. Operating an automobile in Paris was a luxury and if business didn't pick up soon, Larry wouldn't be able to afford the car. He emphatically told Seth, "I work hard to feed this taxi gasoline, but the taxi business does not even put enough food on my table."

Larry continued to bemoan his troubles during the entire drive to Interpol. Seth injected a few "uh-huhs" occasionally to appear as if he were intent on Larry's diatribe of misfortune, but he was really enjoying the ride through the streets of Paris. He didn't know how much longer he would be in Paris and he wanted to absorb every scene. The taxi pulled in front of a very old gray stone office building that housed the offices of Interpol. To Seth, the building seemed to exude mystery and intrigue. He was once again in the realm of imagination, vicariously playing the role of Charlie Chan's "number one son". He wondered where the investigation would lead and if a journey to another part of the world would be imminent.

Seth thanked Larry for the ride and said he would manage to find his own way back to the hotel. As he approached the office door at Interpol, slowing ascending the steps, he reinforced his thoughts of the previous evening and the method of questioning Inspector LeCleur. His thoughts were sharp with excitement of "playing investigator". His appointment had been confirmed with Inspector LeCleur's secretary that morning; and much to his surprise, he was escorted into Inspector LeCleur's office immediately.

"Well, young man, I understand from my secretary that you have an urgent request that has something to do with a missing young woman. How is Interpol involved and how may I help you?" Asked Inspector LeCleur. The Inspector pointed to a chair for Seth to be seated as he sat down on the edge of his desk.

LeCleur studied Seth for a moment; broke the silence and jovially said, "I know who I am, but I don't know if I have your name correctly, young man. My secretary doesn't understand English very well and wasn't able to get the spelling of your name over the phone." The Inspector extended his hand to Seth, smiled and asked, "With whom do I have the pleasure of speaking?"

Seth shook LeCleur's hand and tried not to wince under the pressure of the Inspector's grasp. Seth quickly surmised LeCleur was a strong, powerful man and one you wanted to count as a friend. He was quite tall, rather portly, but whose facial lines denoted a jovial

Riding the Tail of the Dragon

disposition. His large frame was in great contrast to his gentle manner. He looked to be older than Seth had expected, which was, perhaps, due to the War years' taking their toll.

"My name is Seth Coleman and I'm from the U.S.A. Thanks for seeing me on such short notice. The young woman I'm looking for is my half-sister and the trail ends at Interpol in the fall of 1945," Seth stammered. Seth felt a little intimidated by the over-powering stature of the Inspector's size. "There are so many questions...I hardly know where to begin."

"1945," queried LeCleur. He arose from sitting on the front edge of the desk and slowly turned to a leather chair behind his desk. He reached for a cigar, offered one to Seth, who shrugged it off, and proceeded to execute a ritual of preparing the cigar for smoking. He produced a small pocket knife from his trousers and began to whittle a wooden matchstick to just the right size and then inserted it into one end of the cigar. Seth was fascinated by this routine, as he recalled watching his grandfather laboriously fondle a cigar in like manner. Seth attributed the action to that of a gentleman who indulged in smoking, but with a touch of finesse as the cigar was held in the mouth by the matchstick. For a brief moment, Seth's thoughts were diverted to the Ramsey plantation and the days when he and his grandfather would sit for hours along side the riverbank. Seth realized when he became older, the purpose was not to catch fish, as his grandfather would rarely move his cork and line to entice the fish, but rather to spend the day together and talk about things that were important to a young lad growing up.

"1945," LeCleur repeated. He had worked hard to forget the heinous War and he thought he had managed quite well to cloud his memory of the abominable crimes. He really did not want to conjure up unpleasant images during the day, which in dreams had been destroying his sleep at night. The nightmares were growing farther apart, but he reluctantly admitted to himself that the nightmares would never disappear forever. "Perhaps the best way to tell a story is to start at the beginning," he said.

Seth related the story as he had told it the previous day at the orphanage. As he concluded the story with information furnished by the Mother Superior, he noticed the Inspector was jotting down notes on a notepad.

Jeannine Dahlberg

LeCleur continued to puff on his cigar while reading his notes, and then said, "The Sisters at the orphanage worked miracles in keeping the children safe, clothed and fed. They were an inspiration to me when I would visit them, for to see such cheerfulness in the midst of chaotic circumstances was to see the workings of the hand of God. My visits were in connection with the underground operations, which at times the orphanage was involved as you have learned.

"You have asked how it was that General von Horstmann contacted me. I remember our meeting quite well. The general came to my office one night disguised as a French farmer. It was difficult for me to believe his story of espionage within the high ranks of the German officers, but I knew it to be true. As Inspector, I was privy to classified information intercepted at the German headquarters at Versailles; and General Erik von Horstmann, along with many other high-ranking officers, was suspected of being one of the conspirators in the attempt to kill Hitler. SS troops and the Gestapo were everywhere...combing every nook and cranny for anyone even slightly suspected of knowing about the assassination plot. He explained Mother Maria Teresa was hiding Frau Horstmann and Rachel in the orphanage and it was now imperative that he also seek refuge."

LeCleur took a few moments to re-light his cigar and continued. "That night was a night of testimony for both the general and me. Have you ever met someone and realized right away your personalities and principles coincide?" LeCleur asked Seth, but not wanting an answer. "We both experienced the feeling and exchanged stories as if we were old friends. A fabric of friendship was woven that night that would last for many months. I think we were both seeking civility and a reason to forget, if only for a few hours, the devastation of the War-torn countries and the excessive cruelty displayed so blatantly upon the people. There we were: two men...a Frenchman and a German talking congenially for hours; forgetting we were enemies."

Cigar smoke filled the room, reminding Seth of an opium den as portrayed in a Charlie Chan movie. His eyes started to smart from the smoke, but he sat quietly, coughed a little, but said nothing. LeCleur noticed Seth's discomfort, opened the window a little bit more and continued puffing on his cigar.

Riding the Tail of the Dragon

"General von Horstmann asked me for the name of a compatriot of the French Resistance, as he had vital information he would exchange for his safety. He reinforced his request by saying he would join the underground movement until a safe passage was arranged for Frau Horstmann, Rachel and him to leave the country.

"I, of course, was most anxious to learn what information would be so important that would provide sanction to a German general, and I suggested I personally would take him to the underground headquarters for an interview. A meeting was arranged for daybreak the following morning.

"Caution was observed. The general was blindfolded and led through the labyrinth of catacombs of ancient quarries under Paris that served as headquarters for the French Resistance.

"With bold audacity, showing no fear whatsoever, he faced the Frenchmen as calmly as he would confront one of his subordinates. He told of an assassination plot on Churchill's life…laid the plan out in great detail and suggested how to thwart the attack. The attempt on Churchill's life was to be three days hence and he advised preparations should be made immediately and he would actively assist.

"The plan seemed so absurd to all of us at the underground headquarters that we figured it had to be true. It took us four hours to transmit our coded messages through to the Brits and to receive their response. The Brits were aware of some of the details, but not all, and General von Horstmann confided the missing link in the scheme."

LeCleur paused for a moment to ask Seth if he would enjoy a cup of espresso; Seth agreed to a cup and LeCleur continued the story.

"The general was a brave man and proved to be a tremendous asset to the underground resistance. His knowledge of the German army's tactical movements was invaluable. And I suppose the Mother Superior praised his benevolence and shrewdness in being able to obtain food that was in short supply and cart it away to the orphanage. Indeed, he was remarkable."

LeCleur thumped his pencil on the notepad; looked at Seth and continued. "A month or so after D-Day, and as promised, safe passage was arranged for the general, Frau Horstmann and their daughter." The inspector again glanced at his notepad and asked,

"Do you have the note with you that Rachel wrote to the Sisters at the orphanage? You mentioned the general said he had made arrangements to escape to South America, but you said the postmark on the note bears the stamp of Macau."

Seth produced the note from his jacket and handed it to LeCleur. The Inspector carefully looked at the postmark. "Yes, that is correct," LeCleur said. "The French compatriots felt it best that the general tell his family that they would escape to South America if there were a need to divert attention from the real destination…which was Macau. Since Macau belongs to Portugal and Portugal was neutral during the War, Macau became a refuge for escapees from the Japanese. To my knowledge the general and his family arrived safely and, of course, this note bears proof of that." The Inspector lowered his voice and said, "Seth, I guess that is as far as I can take you in your quest to find Rachel. Perhaps, someone in Macau will be able to tell you more."

Seth drained the last sip of espresso and placed the empty cup on the desk; expressed his thanks to Inspector LeCleur for the information and bid him good day. It was a short, productive visit.

Seth literally skipped down the steps two at a time, whistling an up-beat rendition of Sentimental Journey as he stepped into the street to hail a taxi to return to the hotel.

CHAPTER SIX

"Hey, Seth, ol' man, where have you been this morning?" John called from behind the hotel registration desk. "Sarah told us all about your trip to the orphanage yesterday. She was quite taken with the story Mother Superior told and would like to help out more if you need her."

"You, Diedre and Sarah have already been a great help to me. I really appreciate your concern and friendship. My hope of finding Rachel was really bolstered today after talking with Inspector Claude LeCleur. It appears, though, the investigation will take me to Macau, but first I have to find a cheap way to get there," Seth said thoughtfully. "Do you have any ideas, John?"

"Well, how about a slow boat to China," John mused. "Remember that song? I sure do like the American tunes. That's one thing I miss over here is hearing the hit parade. Seriously, Seth, a boat ride would be the cheapest way to travel; if you could book passage on a tramp steamer that would be even cheaper. You may be able to catch one out of Le Havre."

"John, I'm really broke. My dad is going to send a few bucks, but that will take a few days. Any ideas how I can get from here to Le Havre?" Seth asked.

"Oh, sure. Larry will probably be glad to drive you in his taxi for just the cost of the gas. I bet he'd jump at the chance for an excuse to get away from Paris for awhile. I understand from him the taxi business is slow right now. I'll have Sarah ask him to drive you. He'll do anything for Sarah; or haven't you noticed," John chuckled.

"That would be great, John. Now all I have to do is convince my dad to send me enough money for a trip to the Orient. That may not be so easy. John, would you try to get a call through to my dad and I'll soon find out if this investigation will continue," Seth said.

While Seth sat in the lobby waiting for his call to go through, Sarah popped through the door with her hair bouncing on her shoulders. She noticed Seth right away and called to him.

"Seth, you're just the guy I want to see." She opened her purse and handed several pictures to him. "Mother Superior gave these

Jeannine Dahlberg

pictures to me today. She thought they may help you in your search to find Rachel."

Seth took the pictures and closely looked at them. They were pictures cut out of magazines and newspapers depicting General von Horstmann and his family in Berlin at various outings and social functions in Germany. Rachel was clearly noticeable in all the pictures.

"Thanks, Sarah, and be sure to thank Mother Superior. I know these are some of her treasured mementos and I appreciate her sharing them with me. They will come in handy when I'm in Macau."

"Macau!" Sarah exclaimed. "My gosh, you're going to Macau? Where is it anyway?"

"If I remember my geography correctly, it's pretty close to Hong Kong. I found out from Inspector LeCleur today that the island was neutral during the War and served as a refuge for escapees who successfully eluded the Japanese. And, that's where the general took his family." A rush of thoughts passed through his mind. He continued, "I hope dad will send some money so I can stay with the investigation. I really have good vibes about the whole thing, now."

Seth continued to study the pictures. It was easy to see that Rachel lived her young years in an environment of affluence. Seth thought how cruel it was that her lifestyle changed so drastically when she and her mother hid in the orphanage. He shrugged his shoulders and thought…at least it was a "living existence" where otherwise they easily could have been killed by Hitler's Gestapo.

The phone rang and Seth jumped to his feet as John handed him the receiver.

"Hello, dad, I have some good news. I have it on good authority that Rachel is in Macau…well, that's where her note was postmarked."

"Macau!" yelled BillyJoe. That's half way 'round the world! I don't know if I can come up with enough cash to let you go there. How would you get there?" BillyJoe asked.

"Hopefully, I can catch a tramp steamer out of Le Havre, France, which could take me to Macau. I can get to Le Havre from here pretty cheaply with the help of a friend who has his own automobile. Dad, I really feel good about pursuing this lead. I hate to ask you for more money, but, dad, it's important I keep on Rachel's trail." Seth thought about his financially poor predicament for a moment and decided to plead for money by taking a pathetic approach. He sadly said, "Dad, if it took a dime to cross the ocean, I couldn't go from wave to wave."

That made BillyJoe laugh. "Now, son, I know you're not that destitute. You say you're going to Le Havre? I'll wire some money to you there through Ramsey's affiliation with the Euro-Asia Tobacco Center, which is located near the wharf. You should have it in a few days. Be careful, and call me when you find out what tramp steamer you will be boarding."

"Okay, dad, I'll keep in touch."

Seth's contagious jubilation was evident as he spun around to see John and Sarah smile with approval for his impending voyage to Macau. They had listened to Seth's half of the phone conversation and were equally excited.

"Oh, man, you've got a real adventure ahead of you, Seth," marveled John. "The thrill of traveling to the Orient aboard a tramp steamer makes my skin crawl with jealousy." John's happiness changed quickly to groveling in his own self pity. "I think working behind this desk is beginning to feel like a shackle on my ankles. If I didn't love my little woman so much, I'd ask if you would like some company." John winked at Sarah, put his arm around her shoulders and with a slight hug said, "Sarah has been like a daughter to me, and Diedre makes me a happy man. I don't know why I torture myself with thoughts of quitting the hotel business. That burr stings me once in awhile and I get edgy. Then I think of the good life I have here and everything else fades into oblivion. I guess it's my cycle of life."

John snapped out of his philosophical trance and blurted, "We're goin' a miss you 'round here, ol' man. You've added some excitement to this old, mundane hotel. I hope you'll let us know if you find Rachel."

Sarah was quick to add, "I've really had fun and kind of got caught up in this whole investigative thing, too. Will you drop us a note or something if you find her?"

"Of course. I don't know from what corner of the world the postmark will read, but I'll keep in touch. You all have been great and I can't thank you enough for your help." Seth replied. "There is

Jeannine Dahlberg

one thing more, though, Sarah. And that is, would you ask Larry to drive me to Le Havre. Do you think he'll do it?"

"No problem," Sarah hastened to reply. "Larry is probably chomping at the bit for something to do. I know he'll jump at the chance to get out of Paris for a while because the taxi business is really lousy right now. When do you want to leave?" Sarah asked.

"Tomorrow morning, if possible," Seth answered.

With a wave of her hand, Sarah started for the door and called, "I'll let you know tonight after I talk to Larry."

John suggested, "I may as well tally the account for your room as long as I have the books in front of me. How about if we settle up at dinner tonight at my house. Sarah and Larry will be there and we can enjoy your last night in Paris over a bottle of port wine. We'll have two celebrations: One for your good fortune and one for the French compatriots," John explained. "Heard today wine won't be rationed anymore. Hallelujah! See I knew there was a God in heaven to take care of us little people. Even if it is 'baptized', that's to say, watered down and vapid, it still fills the void to quench a man's thirst. It's His little blessings I appreciate." John winked at Seth and exclaimed, "I'll call Diedra and ask her to set one more place at the table. Okay?"

"Sounds great to me," Seth replied.

*****

The morning breeze gently wafting in from the open window was refreshing. Seth continued resting in bed with his head on his folded hands and gazed at great length at the one picture in his hotel room. A slight smile escaped his closed lips. He recognized the figure in the picture to be the infamous Kilroy...as in "Kilroy was here". The figure was known the world over as it was the trademark of the fighting GIs...the half-moon face with two large eyes and a very large nose looking over a fence. Seth knew John was the artist of the whimsical figure in the drawing as they had discussed its significance at great length one evening over a cup of espresso. It was a reminder to John of his small part in a very large war. He belonged to a group of heroes, the invading American GIs who, with the allied forces, liberated the people from oppression and persecution. Seth felt fortunate for having met John and greatly admired his work in helping the people of Paris restore the immediate environs to its historical beauty.

Seth took his time dressing. He was in no hurry. He wondered if his and John's path would ever cross again. He had become a good friend and regretted leaving Paris for that reason. He packed his bags, took a long look around the small, but adequate, room and paused at the door. He couldn't resist. He pulled a pencil from atop the dresser, walked to the Kilroy picture and scribbled at the bottom, "and so was I".

Larry was parked at the curb waiting for Seth; and after more good-byes to John and Diedra, the two set off for Le Havre.

Jeannine Dahlberg

CHAPTER SEVEN

"Gasoline. That's going to be just one of my worries on this trip," lamented Larry. "And then there's that left rear tire. It has so many patches on the tube...and a boot in the tire...and..." Larry's sentence trailed off. "Le Havre isn't that far, maybe two hundred kilometers, but it may just take us all day to get there. If I don't hit too many ruts in the road, we may be all right.

"Your quick decision to go to Le Havre didn't give me much time to get the extra gasoline coupons I'll need for this trip," Larry blurted. "I was up most the night trying to contact my friend, Paul, who helps me out once in awhile when I need gasoline. I don't know how you fellas operate in the States, but in France gasoline is still rationed and sometimes even the taxi drivers have to rely on black-market coupons."

Seth felt it was too early in the morning for this in-depth conversation. He had just hopped into the taxi and Larry was already expounding upon his predicament. Over the last few days, Seth had learned, however, that Larry was prone to talk at great length on any topic. He was beginning to think Larry would make a grand orator, and maybe, he would have something to contribute to the French diplomatic corps.

Seth retorted, "Rationing was pretty tough in the States during the War, but now nothing is rationed...some things are just hard to get. We were always running out of meat coupons. I can remember eating cuts of meat for dinner where I wasn't too certain what kind of an animal it came from. I've always had a big appetite and I guess I felt the effects of rationing more in my stomach. Now, Dad had trouble getting tires for the tractors on the plantation, but there was always enough gas to run the equipment. He always said thank goodness the Ramsey name still had clout in Washington, and the tobacco fields never suffered from lack of care."

"Well, I guess I shouldn't complain as much as I do about gasoline rationing," Larry responded. "We, taxi drivers, get our share. Most others have to depend entirely upon black-market coupons from the Brittany fishing ports. Those poor commercial fishermen make more money by selling their gasoline coupons than

40

by operating their gasoline-powered motorboats so they can fish. In fact, Paul gave me the name of a fisherman where I can stop to pick up a few coupons on the way back to Paris so I can get this ol' jalopy home. Seth, I sure hope you have enough cash on you to buy them. I sure don't."

Seth was in a reflective mood, half listening to Larry, and started laughing. "I was just thinking," he said. "Did you have as much trouble as we did getting shoes? I still remember the soles of my shoes flapping. I used to act like a tap dancer...like Bojangles. Once, some of my classmates and I worked up a silly routine and danced in a school minstrel show. Those were some fun times...at least we made the best of a serious situation."

There was a quiet time in the taxi that followed, as both conjured up thoughts of life during the War. Both felt the effects of the War, but both related to it differently. Larry remembered each day as being a challenge to survive in a daily life-threatening situation. There was nothing of the War or rationing that conjured up anything remotely funny. There were no happy interludes.

Seth answered Larry's concern for money to pay for the black-market gasoline coupons and explained his dad was going to wire money to him at Le Havre.

Both fell silent as the taxi continued to motor to the coast; both realized they could not relate to each other's war experiences.

The morning sun illuminated the fields to a pristine beauty. Hedgerows were trimmed once again and ditches were cleaned of debris. The countryside was looking like its old, beautiful self. It was difficult to envision these beautiful fields as a battleground. Larry noticed some farmers were still taking advantage of German-prisoner farm labor.

By mid-afternoon, the air was pungent with the smell of the sea as they were nearing the beaches of Normandy. It wouldn't be much farther and they would be in Le Havre.

Larry began talking incessantly about the bloody battles of Normandy. Seth, of course, was well aware of the Normandy invasion, but he decided to let Larry vent his anger and frustration over the futility of war.

Seth thought: *Here I go again; I'm in for another long discourse.*

Seth listened as Larry outlined his hope for a reconstructed France that would hail its glorious beauty. A beauty that would encompass a socio-economic lifestyle worthy of France's compatriots. As he expatiated longer on his desire for France, his solemn vow became a requiem for those who died saving France.

He became even more determined to finish his studies at the university, and his compelling desire to work in the diplomatic corps was now stronger than ever. Larry knew the elections next spring would determine the fate of France politically, economically and socially and he wanted to be an integral part of the "new" France. Inflation would have to be curbed; politics were dangerously fragile and problems of strikes against the utilities had to be solved. Perhaps, General de Gaulle would be France's savior.

As the taxi pulled into Le Havre, Seth's anomalous attitude toward Larry changed, as he now admired his enthusiasm and determination to succeed as a diplomat. Experiencing the ravages of war first hand definitely had given Larry an edge on maturity. Larry's serious congenital fears and concerns for the national morality and stability of France strengthened his fiber of sensibility. Seth realized Larry's desire to become a diplomat was as strong as his desire to become an architect. Both wanted to build their countries to greatness. Both had the energy and naiveté of youth.

As they pulled into the port town, Larry explained that ninety percent of Le Havre had been destroyed in the War. Its close proximity to Great Britain's coast (across the English Channel) made Le Havre a target of many bombings by the RAF.

They were surprised to see that so much of the city had been restored, and Seth was extremely happy to see the harbor and wharf area in adequate repair.

As they looked out across the harbor, shipping vessels of all sizes and shapes were casting long shadows on the water giving an illusion of an even busier harbor. Seth scanned the vessels in hopes of finding a tramp steamer…one which would take him to Macau. First, it was necessary to find a hotel for the night.

CHAPTER EIGHT

What a grand, glorious day Seth thought as he opened his eyes to see the harbor bustling with activity. Larry was still sleeping as the rigors of the drive the previous day left him quite exhausted. Two flat tires were enough; but when the third tire blew out, that was a little too much. Seth became a little weary and frustrated with the ordeal, but Larry's exuberant personality didn't waiver on the whole trip nor did his incessant conversation. Seth was determined to give him a large tip for all his trouble, besides buying the black-market gasoline coupons.

Seth was anxious to find the office of the Euro-Asia Tobacco Company to find out if his dad had wired him the money...and how much. He purposely made noise dressing so Larry would be awakened.

With one eye open, Larry could see and feel Seth's enthusiasm to get started. Larry wasn't as eager to get up, as he knew this day would bring an end to a relationship that had blossomed into an exciting adventure. Larry envied Seth's impending journey to Macau and the excitement of not knowing what to expect. He wondered if he would ever find Rachel.

There was no problem finding the business office of the tobacco company as the building and surrounding storage area consumed a large portion of land along the wharf.

Larry waited outside the office.

Seth was euphoric as he burst through the office door and called to Larry, "Sometimes dad is really great! I have enough money to get me to Macau and then some. He's anxious for me to continue my search for Rachel." Seth thought to himself...*albeit there are times when he makes me feel frustrated*...and in even deeper contemplation...*is Rachel really my half-sister? And, if so, why didn't dad tell me.*

Seth pulled Larry aside from the pedestrian traffic on the boardwalk and placed his hand on Larry's arm.

"I want you to take this money," Seth said as he pressed the bills into Larry's hand.

Jeannine Dahlberg

Larry looked at the wad of bills and exclaimed, "Good heavens, this is manna from heaven...and so much. Seth, are you sure you want to give me all this?"

"I should say I do," Seth replied. "The cost of gasoline, the wear and tear on your taxi, your time and certainly the physical work of changing all the flat tires...not to mention the good companionship...Larry, maybe it's not enough."

"My gosh, man, this will even pay for some of my books next semester. I don't know how to thank you."

"You don't have to. It is I who want to thank you. I only wish we had an opportunity to get to know one another better and to become close friends. You have such a vast knowledge of so many really important matters that I feel I have learned a lot from you. Perhaps, one day, when you are a great statesman and I am a prosperous architect, we will meet again to sit down and reminisce about our motor trip from Paris to Le Havre."

Seth turned away from Larry and glanced out over the harbor.

"Well, Larry, I guess my next plan of action is to find a tramp steamer that will take me to Macau. I kind of hate to say good-bye, so let's just say, so long."

The two young men clasped each other, wondering, in fact, if they would ever meet again.

Riding the Tail of the Dragon

CHAPTER NINE

With a quick step, Seth hurried to the steamship office to book passage on the first tramp steamer going to Macau. The boardwalk was already crowded with pedestrians, workmen and seamen, and the whole general area was still under construction. Longshoremen at the wharf were hustling to load the many ships anchored at the dock and in the harbor.

Seth believed he was quite knowledgeable when it came to sailing. He and some school friends would take the Ramsey sailboat out to sea once in awhile, but he certainly didn't consider himself a salt-of-the-sea sailor.

Some of the ships anchored in the harbor looked rather old, rusty and intimidating. His imagination conjured up scenes from the many books he had read and from the many movies he had seen about the sea. He had a passion for adventure stories, but his thoughts were becoming too dark and foreboding and he quickly put them out of his mind. He didn't want these thoughts to be a portent of happenings to come. He definitely did not want the captain of his ship, though, to be another Captain Bligh or Captain Ahab. He was beginning to feel apprehensive about the impending voyage to Macau. Once again, his adrenaline was pumping as he entered the steamship office.

For a new office building, the facade had the appearance of an old eighteenth century structure, perhaps it had been restored to convey the charm of the building that had been destroyed.

As he entered the large room, he noticed placards posted on a huge bulletin board. The master of each vessel listed the ports of call. Seth surmised from reading the many placards that a tramp steamer would sail to ports and places in any part of the world as the master may direct, returning to the port of discharge for a term of time not to exceed twelve months. Hence, the list of ports was quite extensive and covered many seas all over the world. One placard specifically mentioned Macau...the *S/S Ladybug*. And it could carry three passengers. It was scheduled to sail in two days.

Seth learned that the *S/S Ladybug* was an old tramp steamer that had been powered by steam and recently converted to diesel engine. It was of Swedish registry with a competent master...and best of all he could book passage. He hoped it would not take six months to get to Macau. He didn't want to miss a full year before starting his career as an architect.

Seth put the ticket and boarding pass in his pocket and asked to use the phone for an overseas call. The ticket agent was reluctant at first, but Seth pulled out a few U.S. dollars, handed them to the agent who in turn handed the phone to Seth. Seth was learning the power of the American dollar.

*****

"Dad, I'm in Le Havre and I've booked passage on the *S/S Ladybug* bound for Macau and other ports. Of course, you know, a tramp steamer goes wherever there is cargo to be shipped, so I may see quite a bit of the world before I reach Macau."

"Son, can you afford the trip? Did I wire you enough money?" BillyJoe inquired.

"You were more than generous, dad. I'll either call you or send you a telegram from our first port of call. Wish me luck in finding Rachel."

"Son, take care. The Orient has always held a mystical fascination for me and I want you to be very careful. Don't take any chances," BillyJoe warned.

"Dad, don't worry. I won't do anything you wouldn't do," Seth chuckled.

"That's what I'm afraid of." With that BillyJoe hung up the phone, sat down at the table and put his head in his hands. He was worried. Seth was his only son, and he was going to experience a culture shock beyond his wildest dreams.

CHAPTER TEN

Lightning cracked across the sky orchestrating rumblings in ominous gray/green clouds. Fierce wind ripped the water changing sea swells into gigantic waves which crashed against the *S/S Ladybug*. The tender, which ferried Seth and the other two passengers from the shore to the *Ladybug*, had great difficulty negotiating the waves. Seth wondered what propelled the urgency to board the passengers on the ship during a storm. He trusted the captain had a very good reason.

As the tender pulled along side the *Ladybug* so the three passengers could embark, a cold chill went through Seth's body. The ship rocked rampageously as the three slowly and carefully ascended the lowered plank and rope ladder. The *Ladybug* was an old ship with a rather small pilothouse. Seth was not too happy with the size of the ship and was hoping for a much bigger and better maintained vessel. He counted about a dozen men scurrying on deck to secure hatch covers and the cargo hold against the strong wind and heavy sea. The captain came forward to greet the passengers and then quickly turned to attend to the immediate care of his ship and its cargo.

Seth quickly surmised after seeing the stern, intimidating demeanor of the captain that he was a man who would be in total control of any situation. Seth's quick imagination cloaked the captain in a Viking's raiment and he decided not to question the captain's reasoning for boarding the ship during a storm.

All three passengers were quickly escorted below deck and were asked to remain in their cabins for safety reasons until the storm subsided. Long afternoon hours took their toll on Seth's nausea. Finally, the storm clouds rolled out and the sea became quite calm. The three were advised the ship would leave port with the tide as scheduled. Seth left his cabin for a walk on the deck, hoping the fresh air would relieve his queasy feeling. The brilliant colors of orange and yellow as they streaked across the sky at the horizon where the sea and the sky become one were spectacular. He could see the mouth of the Seine River where it entered at Le Havre and his thoughts quickly turned to his friends in Paris and the leisurely afternoon he spent along the river. He would never forget Paris.

Captain Leif Oscarson invited the three passengers to sit at his table to eat during the voyage. He was quite cordial, which mannerism was definitely in contrast to his rough, burly appearance.

Seth sat quietly at the dinner table, more looking at the food than eating it. He didn't remember ever being seasick when he and his friends would test their skills against the fickleness of Mother Nature while sailing along the Virginia coastline. His stomach was still playing havoc with his appetite and he hoped the uncomfortable feeling would leave him soon. Captain Oscarson was quiet, also. His enigmatic disposition left Seth with a rather cold and unpleasant feeling that he considered the passengers an imposition. The other two passengers were dominating the conversation, mostly about the terrible storm and the wild ride on the tender.

Both passengers expressed their concern for Seth and his inability to enjoy the fine meal prepared for their first night at sea. He politely acknowledged their sympathy, but chose to remain quiet. He lapsed into the game of trying to identify his traveling companions' lifestyles and occupations.

He studied the woman first. She was rather glib in speech and her sentences did not always parse. In fact, at times her thoughts rambled and were incoherent; but it was quite evident, she wanted to control the conversation. She quickly divulged her whole life history during the course of dinner: she was born in Germany, named for her grandmother Lily and was educated in Britain. She was traveling to China to become a missionary on the island of Lantau, which was not too far from Hong Kong. It seemed to Seth she wanted to keep no secrets. She discussed her life as if it were an open book and left nothing for Seth to question or wonder about her life.

When Seth turned his attention to the other passenger, Andre Reuter, he was not quick to surmise his character. He was a short, wiry fellow with big, thick glasses. His small, penetrating eyes did not appear to focus clearly, but his movements were quick and vigorous as if compensating for his myopic vision. He said he lived in Holland and was traveling to the Orient on business. Seth studied Andre for some time and could not begin to imagine his line of business. His facial expressions were in contrast to his mannerisms

Riding the Tail of the Dragon

as if what he said did not coincide with his true feelings. The more Andre talked, the more Seth felt ill at ease about his true character.

Their dinner was interrupted when they heard loud voices in the passageway outside the dining room. The captain bolted from his chair to see what the disturbance was. Two seamen were in the corridor angrily discussing the cargo. The captain grabbed each man by the arm and quickly escorted them out of earshot of the dining room.

Seth thought he could hear something being said about the rough sea and the timber not being secured properly in the hold. Seth knew the ship had taken on its cargo the previous two days in port, but he did not know what the ship was carrying or to what destination. The captain had told the passengers earlier that he would inform them of their first destination stop at dinner.

When the captain returned to the dining room, he appeared agitated. He apologized for the disturbance and informed the passengers there was no reason for concern. He explained the cargo had shifted in the hold because of the weight and roll of the elm timbers the ship was transporting to Macau, which was to be the ship's third destination port after Panama and Hong Kong.

"I have had great difficulty in recruiting seasoned sailors lately," the captain lamented. "They're an adventurous sort who want to see the world, but they wouldn't give a plug nickel to learn the art of being a crafted seaman. I suppose the experienced sailors had their fill of excitement on the seas during the War and are now content to have their feet on solid ground."

"Captain, if you don't mind my asking, you appear to be awfully young to have your own ship...cargo or otherwise. Did you serve in the navy during the War and where was your loyalty...I mean, was your sympathy with Hitler or the Western Allies?" questioned Andre.

"Well, sir, the War is over and there is no need to test loyalties, now. I will tell you that I am from Scandinavia and mighty proud of it. All the men in my family were fishermen and so I learned my way around a ship and the sea at a very early age. The War exacted its share of grief on my family and I am now the only one who sails the seas. I know my craft well." Slowly, and somewhat distracted, the captain added, "I had good teachers."

Jeannine Dahlberg

Lily was happy to learn that Hong Kong would be the *Ladybug's* second stop and asked the captain, "Do you think I will have a problem finding someone to take me to Lantau from Hong Kong?"

To the surprise of his table companions, the captain laughed uproariously. "When the Chinese find out you will pay in British currency for transportation to Lantau, every Chinese junk and sampan will be in Victoria Harbor eagerly waiting to carry you across the Pearl River Estuary. Someone may even get you there safely." The captain's expression then became quite serious and he cautioned, "Perhaps, I will be able to assist you at that time to see that you choose the right one. You must be very careful traveling alone. Do you own a handgun?"

With that question, Seth thought Lily would faint. He felt she must have led a cloistered life up to now if she didn't realize the danger of traveling alone in the Orient. Then Seth quickly thought of his own predicament. He did not give any previous thought to his own safety. He would make it a point to discuss his traveling plans with the captain privately and as soon as possible. His dad's warning to be careful took on a new meaning.

After coffee and dessert, the captain excused himself from the table, saying he had much paperwork to complete before retiring, but he suggested the others remain in the dining room for conversation or cards. Seth thought, evidently, the dining room was also to be used as the parlor or recreation room.

Before the three passengers could arise from the table, Lily took the opportunity to ask Seth his reason for traveling to the Orient. He was about to respond when he glanced at Andre and noted the alert expression on his face, his beady eyes and his twisted little mouth, as if eagerly awaiting Seth's answer. Seth felt bad vibrations going through his body and he decided right then he did not like or trust Andre.

"I'm going to Macau to oversee the operation of our tobacco warehouse to determine if we want to continue serving Mainland China from Macau or perhaps move the warehouse to another location," Seth reported.

Lily questioned, "Where did you say you are from?"

"I'm from the fine tobacco state of Virginia," Seth answered with pride.

"Well, how come you boarded this tramp steamer in Le Havre?" Lily queried.

Seth replied, "I just graduated college and decided to bum around Europe for awhile this summer before starting my job in the fall. Then my dad asked if I would like to check our tobacco warehouse in Macau before returning to the States and I jumped at the chance."

Seth felt quite happy with his reply. He decided it would be prudent not to reveal the real reason for his journey to Macau. He recognized he was naive in worldly matters, but his eyes were opened during the conversation at the dinner table. He did not know the captain or the other two passengers and his mission to find Rachel and her family was definitely no one's business. Seth knew Rachel and her family were in hiding from someone and he was not going to divulge any information, which may jeopardize their safety.

"Andre, how about you? Do you feel the need to carry a handgun while traveling on your business trips to the Orient?" Lily asked.

"Oh, my no!" Andre quickly responded. "I have never liked violence and have never owned a gun. I travel around the world in search of very fine textiles and silk fabrics, and buy and sell to many of the well-known fashion designers in Europe. Perhaps you own an evening gown made of an exquisite silk fabric that I selected. I prefer the more genteel lifestyle."

That was a rather plausible answer Seth acknowledged, but there was something about Andre that was not believable. His personality and appearance did not coincide with the sharp, gregarious personality of a salesman. Perhaps it was the combination of the twitch at the corner of his mouth plus the stare of his eyes and the constant cigarette in his hand that reminded Seth of some of the gangster movies he had seen with Sydney Greenstreet, Peter Lori and James Cagney. In any event, Seth decided to avoid Andre as much as possible while on the ship.

The ship's bell rang ten o'clock and the three simultaneously decided to turn in for the night. They could feel the rock of the ship as they walked together down the corridor to their rooms. Seth's room was located between the other two passenger rooms. As he bid each a pleasant good night, Seth noticed a slight bulge in Andre's coat when it snagged on a bolt at the doorframe. Andre quickly jerked the coat from the snag and went into his room. Seth's first thought was that Andre was concealing a gun under his coat, but he admonished himself for letting his imagination get out of hand. He would have to quit playing the inscrutable detective and settle down to reality. Lily noticed the incident also, but said nothing.

    Seth lay on his bunk bed waiting for sleep to come for what seemed an eternity, but the roll of the ship and the waves slapping against its hull was not conducive to sleep. The ship's bell rang out the hour many times and he was still punching his pillow trying to get into a sleep-inducing position. He could not stop thinking of the events of the day: the dangerous ride on the tender in a fierce storm, his traveling companions and the elusive captain. The cabin walls were quite thin and, as if by schedule, Seth could hear Andre in his cabin coughing more often than the toll of the ship's bell.

    It was past three o'clock in the morning. Between his mind racing with random thoughts and the queasy feeling still in his stomach, Seth decided to go on deck to get some fresh air.

    He quietly opened his cabin door so as not to disturb anyone. Andre was still coughing periodically, but there was no light streaming from under his door. Seth concluded, he must cough in his sleep. Lily's room was quiet.

    The ship appeared to rock more as he slowly made his way down the dimly lit corridor. He hoped there was not going to be another storm. He noticed a light shining through the crack at the threshold of the captain's door and Seth could hear low, muffled voices. His ambiguous thoughts played havoc with his sense of propriety, but curiosity won and he leaned gently against the door. The captain's voice was easily distinguishable as it was low and resonant; and there was no question that the second voice belonged to a woman…and that had to be Lily.

    As he stood at the door trying not to breathe so he could hear better, Seth wondered if this were a clandestine rendezvous between the two. A pang of guilt ran through his body. If the two were having an affair, it was certainly none of his business. He was about ready to leave when he heard more clearly some of the dialogue. They were talking about the cargo…something about certain elm timbers, which had been hollowed out and plugged with gold bullion. Seth did not know whether to linger longer and hear more or run

Riding the Tail of the Dragon

away from the illicit scheme being discussed. His curiosity surpassed good judgment and he pushed harder against the door.

"What was the lame-brain idea of having the three of us board the ship during a storm. I'd like to live through this episode of my life. Who knows what lies ahead of us." Lily asserted.

"I don't feel the need to explain my actions to you." barked the captain.

"We're in this together to the end and if you want my full cooperation, you'll have to tell me what's going on." Lily spoke with such authority that Seth couldn't believe this was the same woman who spoke so frivolously at the dinner table.

"I suppose you're right," the captain admitted. "We are all going to have to pull together on this one if it's going to go down. It was urgent that the *Ladybug* sails on schedule so we can be in Macau on the appointed date. I will anchor briefly in Victoria Harbor so you can continue your journey to Lantau. The general is most eager for your arrival. Everything has been set in motion to welcome you as the new missionary. I think your guise this evening at dinner was convincing. The young man from the states seems innocent enough, but Andre bears watching."

Lily spoke in a soft, low whisper, which caused Seth to push even harder against the door.

"Andre was concealing a gun inside his coat jacket this evening," said Lily.

"Are you sure?" asked the captain.

"No doubt about it. His coat hooked on a bolt at the doorframe and I saw it. I'm not certain if the young man noticed it," Lily replied.

"Well then, the general was correct in his suspicion of Andre, which means the information that has been forwarded to the general is right on target. He's our quisling. I wonder what induced him to collaborate with the Nazis. I hope we can unload the timber cargo before anyone gets hurt," stated the captain.

Lily spoke emphatically, "Don't worry about Andre. I'll take care of him if need be. You concentrate on your part of this operation."

The ship rolled with such great force that Seth lost his footing and smashed into the wall opposite the captain's door. Flustered and

Jeannine Dahlberg

scared. Seth staggered to his cabin with as much speed as his shaking legs would carry him.

The captain quickly opened his door just in time to see Seth going into his cabin. Lily and the captain quizzically looked at each other. Was it possible he heard any part of their conversation? What was he doing out of his cabin at that time in the morning? They both agreed they would have to find out more about this young man from Virginia.

Seth quickly closed his cabin door behind him and stood there for some time with his back braced against the door. He could not hear footsteps in the hallway so he surmised no one had followed him. His heart was pounding and breathing was difficult. He didn't ever remember being so frightened, not even while playing in the big mansion on the plantation where he imagined the ghost of old man Ramsey walked the halls. He realized that was all pretend, just thoughts to give him a rush of excitement and fear. What he was now experiencing was real fear in a real world and he did not like this new feeling.

When he was certain no one was going to break into his cabin, he dressed for bed. After awhile, he regained his composure and tried to concentrate on his mission at hand. And that is to find Rachel. He lay on his bunk for a long time trying to plan his field of action. To discuss his travel plans with the captain now seemed absurd. He decided to keep a very low profile during the voyage and not get into any in-depth conversations with anyone. He rationalized that no matter what illegal actions were transpiring on the ship, they were not his concern. The events of the day were all too serious and he had no desire to play the inscrutable detective Charlie Chan. It already had cost his dad a lot of money toward the search to locate Rachel, and Seth was not going to let his dad down. He would stay focused; find Rachel and her family and sail for home. The thought of home sounded really good to him. The ship's bell tolled five and with pleasant thoughts of home, Seth drifted off to sleep.

CHAPTER ELEVEN

It was late in the morning when Seth entered the dining room. Breakfast had been served a few hours before, but he hoped to get a cup of coffee. The thought of food still did not appeal to him. He was surprised to see Lily and Andre still sitting in the dining room. Lily sat in a big lounge chair knitting and Andre sat at the card table playing solitaire. There appeared to be no conversation between the two, and Seth thought they simply were keeping an eye on each other. Neither one looked up when Seth sat at the table with his coffee. He welcomed the silence.

Lily was the first to speak. "Well, how is our young traveler, today? I hope you've found your sea legs and can enjoy a hearty breakfast. Look, Andre, don't you think he looks much better? My, you're quite handsome when you're not so green around the gills. I trust you had a good night's rest. I, for one, will be very happy to get off this cargo ship. It certainly lacks amenities. But then, I should have known better than to book passage on a tramp steamer. Of course, the church was happy because it was a much cheaper fare."

Lily rambled on and on; asking questions but expecting no answers. Seth was amazed at the charade she played. He felt she was quite convincing and wondered if Andre bought her guise.

With coffee cup in hand, Seth decided to go on the top deck where he could get some fresh air. He was cordial to the others; mentioned he was still a little queasy and left the dining room. There was no way he wanted to be in their company any longer than needed.

The gentle touch of the sea breeze upon Seth's face rejuvenated his whole body, and he stood at the railing for quite some time in awe of the expanse of the ocean. The ship cut through the water in a rhythmic motion, which no longer disturbed his equilibrium. He watched the deckhands performing their daily chores and he could easily relate to their desire to be sailors. Aside from the hard work involved keeping such a vessel afloat, which was not to his liking, it was the lure of the sea that captivated his imagination. There was a sense of freedom along with an appreciation of the unknown. The depths of the water hold many mysteries and Seth was consumed with the thought of being so insignificant in the Master's plan. He felt

Jeannine Dahlberg

very humble and alone. He stared into the deep blue water, feeling the roll of the ship and the motion of the sea and he was held in an hypnotic trance.

With both forearms braced on the deck railing to offer steady support from the roll of the ship, Seth held the coffee cup, gazing into it as if to seek answers to the perplexing conversation he overheard between the captain and Lily. He feared he had been seen scurrying into his room and, in retrospect, he wished he had not lingered at the captain's door—then he would not be in this predicament. Hindsight did not ease his tension of feeling boxed into a corner with no knowledge of what was happening. He definitely did not want to become involved in the illegal plot being connived by the captain and Lily, and he pondered at great length the crew's excitement and the captain's anxiety regarding the problem of the ship's cargo. Then his thoughts quickly flashed to Andre's concealed weapon. He had no conjectural answers to any one of these serious concerns. He concluded he must stay focused on his reason for going to Macau.

A light spray of water splashed up onto Seth when the bow of the ship dipped deep into a large wave. Seth bolted a little, surprised by the coolness of the water on his face. The suddenness of his reaction cleansed his mind of foreboding speculations, and he was happy for the brief reprieve.

The mood was broken quickly when Seth felt a firm tap on his shoulder. He was startled, lost control of his composure, dropped his coffee cup over the railing and spun around to see Captain Oscarson standing beside him. They both looked overboard to follow the descent of the coffee cup into the dark water at the side of the ship.

"I didn't mean to startle you, Seth. You appeared to be absorbed in concentration. I hope you aren't contemplating jumping overboard. The lure of the sea is magnified when you stare at its depth for too long, as many sailors will attest to—and I don't want to lose a passenger that way," confided the captain.

"I noticed from the ship's record that you have booked passage to Macau. We will anchor in Victoria Harbor for a day or two before we continue our trip up the Pearl River. I want to escort our British passenger to the island of Lantau, as I feel obligated to see that all the ship's passengers arrive at their destination safely. Is this your first trip to China?" asked the captain.

Riding the Tail of the Dragon

"Yes, it is," replied Seth.

"Well, young man, you are in for a real culture shock. Old world modes of thought are bogged down in centuries of traditional existence. Celebrations of rituals and ceremonies are rooted in the past. I believe you will find it interesting to witness this social and economic group of people who are diversely in contrast to peoples in the Western Hemisphere. Western nations are making inroads into their ancient environment and culture, but progress is very slow. The Chinese people are reluctant to accept Western influences, but perhaps with enlightenment and passing of years, they will yield to a desire for progress toward a higher plane of existence." The captain paused for a moment and placed his hand on Seth's arm as if to confide a personal thought. "We are smug to think that the Caucasian race has all the right answers to life in its purest and happiest state." The captain smiled and continued, "How did I ever get off on that tangent."

Both stood at the railing in silence for a few moments, watching the waves break at the bow of the ship. The captain broke the silence and asked, "What brings you to this part of the world? Macau can be a very dangerous place to visit."

"Luck, I guess," Seth retorted. "I was bumming around Europe on vacation before I start to work this fall and my dad asked if I wanted to go to Macau to check on the company's tobacco warehouse before returning to the States. My answer, of course, was—great!" Seth hoped his answer was light hearted enough to satisfy the captain's curiosity for his trip to Macau.

"We will put into port for a few days in Macau while our cargo is transferred to the dock; and if you should need help of any kind, contact me. As I mentioned before, I like my passengers to arrive safely."

The captain's attention was averted to an incident involving two of the new deckhands. It appeared the two did not know the procedure for storing a few of the guide ropes. The captain left Seth to assist and train the new sailors, but turned and asked Seth, "What did you say the name of the tobacco company is in Macau?"

"I didn't mention the name, but it's the Euro-Asia Tobacco Company," Seth answered.

Jeannine Dahlberg

CHAPTER TWELVE

Lily knew she must work as quickly as possible in the radio room to transmit cables to Scotland Yard in London, which would be forwarded to the States, and to Interpol in Paris, as it was now imperative to find out the identity of her traveling companions. The equipment was very old and very slow, which concerned her that it may take longer than anticipated. Her anxiety was alleviated to some extent, however, in knowing that Captain Oscarson called all the sailors on deck to assist with the guide ropes. He planned to detain them for as long a time as needed for Lily to send the cables. Her apprehension in working with the captain also diminished, as she felt a kindled spark that perhaps the captain would make a good partner on this assignment. She smiled to herself and reflected upon her training in the secret service department—training she received so many years ago and which had served her well. She received three commendations from the department for exemplary service while in the field—she was no stranger to danger. She was selected for this assignment because of her experience in dealing with the smuggling of artifacts and gold from war-torn Germany to South America and the Orient. Being fluent in five languages contributed to her being invaluable to the department when it was necessary to converse with people of different nationalities. Espionage, however, was a dangerous business and she always believed it was to her advantage to withhold this knowledge of languages, as more than once her expertise came in handy during nervously tense moments to eavesdrop on a conversation where it was assumed she could not understand the language.

The messages she relayed were short, stating, "Urgent I receive immediately all vital stats on Andre Reuter, traveling on Dutch passport, employed as salesman for Apogee Fabrics, Ltd., Paris, bound for Canton."

Her second message read, "Urgent I receive immediately all vital stats on Seth Coleman, traveling on a United States passport from Virginia bound for Euro-Asia Tobacco Co. in Macau." Using her secret agent name, Lily signed the messages—Sydney. There was no need to send a coded message, but she requested the reply be in code and forwarded to Lily Muench, Missionary, Lantau Island, care of the *S/S Ladybug*. She did not want the contents of the reply message to be understood by the radio operator. She returned the equipment to its proper order, checked the corridor for clearance, and closed the door behind her. She moved quietly and swiftly—careful to avoid contact with anyone—when she spied Andre opening the door into the corridor leading to the cargo hold. Her first thought was to follow him, but the stakes were too high to take a chance at being seen.

Lily made her way to the top deck where Captain Oscarson was commanding all the seamen in their performance of proper ship maintenance. He addressed all the men as if they were first-time sailors, which instruction disgruntled the seasoned sailors. It was, however, necessary to detain all the men in order to give Lily enough time to send the cables. And he rationalized, it would be a good idea to humble the "old salts" as some were expressing a lordly attitude over the new men. There were, in fact, three new men who were brought on board for this specific sailing. All three were under Lily's authority to direct their actions when and if necessary.

Lily assumed Andre must have realized all hands were on deck and decided to make his move on investigating the cargo hold. She knew everyone was accounted for except Seth when she saw him leaning over the railing and wondered if he were still seasick. Captain Oscarson noticed Lily giving him the high sign that she needed to talk to him. He dismissed the men to return to their routine duties.

"Well, my dear, did you send the cables?" queried the captain.

"Yes. Hopefully, we will have our answers quickly." Lily hastened to reply; and added, "Andre's in the cargo hold. He must be extremely worried if he feels he has to locate the timbers bearing the gold and personally verify they are properly secured. The stakes must be high if he is willing to risk being caught."

"Lily, as we discussed, I assigned your men to alternate being stationed in the cargo hold on an eight-hour watch. If Andre tries anything, he will have to tangle with one of your agents."

*****

Andre wasn't known for his sure-footedness. His clumsy actions were attributed partially to his poor eyesight and to his lack of coordination. He stumbled down the ladder to the cargo hold, twisting his ankle and making more noise than he wanted. His ankle appeared to be swelling quickly and he rubbed it vigorously as if to dissipate the swelling, but it was to no avail. He sat on the rung of the ladder longer than good judgment dictated, cursing himself for his clumsiness. He knew he had to locate the marked timbers quickly and he hobbled down the aisles—one after another—until he found the two large elm timbers, which he identified by the small notched markings wedged into the tree rings at the base of the trunk.

His small eyes sparkled with delight as he envisioned the enormous wealth of gold bullion each huge hollowed-out trunk concealed. He was anxious for the timbers to be unloaded in Macau so his part in this smuggling theft could be finished. He had proved his loyalty over and over again to Nazi Germany during the War and he was ready to live a quiet life. His thoughts projected his plan to continue up the Pearl River to Canton where he would disembark the *Ladybug* and would forever be lost in China—well, at least for a few years or for whatever length of time he deemed necessary. He had accumulated enough wealth, which was stashed away in Swiss accounts, so he could live in splendor anywhere he pleased. He realized he would become a maverick—an outcast who would be hunted by countries in the Western Hemisphere; and after resigning from the Association, he would be hunted in Europe. With his knowledge of names of people and incidents involving the theft of millions of dollars in smuggling the booty of War, he knew his life would be in grave jeopardy. He sat mulling these thoughts and surmised that to live somewhere in South America would be the logical choice—perhaps, Argentina. Yes, he would live in Argentina.

Andre was lost in solitary thought when the door opened, startling him to reality. He panicked and crouched low in the aisle so as not to be seen. His ankle was definitely giving him trouble; and with the added weight forced on it by stooping, he let out a groan.

The agent heard the sound, secured the door behind him and braced for action. He started up the first aisle, checking the cargo as he went. He couldn't isolate the sound. Could it have been the chains slipping on the timbers or was it someone in the hold. He wished there were more lights. He didn't realize until now that the hold was so dimly lit.

Riding the Tail of the Dragon

Sweat exuded from the large pores in Andre's face, fogging his glasses, and his ankle throbbed with pain, hampering swift movement. He was fearful of stumbling again in the narrow, dark aisle and slowly and quietly inched his way to the far open-ended corridor. The air was stifling, making breathing difficult. The large stacked timbers, which were secured on each side of the narrow aisle, created a tunnel-like effect, igniting his claustrophobic tendencies. Expletives furiously spewed from his mouth in soft, mumbling, guttural tones as he cursed himself for being so stupid. It would not be prudent for him to be found in the cargo hold—how could he explain his presence to the seaman on duty.

Random thoughts flashed through his mind. The Association forwarded the message to him when he was in Le Havre that the gold would be smuggled in timbers loaded aboard the *Ladybug,* and the code identifying the timbers also was relayed in the message. Why did he feel he had to find the timbers now? The relayed information should have sufficed, but he did not want anything to go wrong with his last job for the Association. It became more imperative that he quit, for he was far too old to see a job of this magnitude to completion. Without question, it was his percentage of the take of gold bullion, which was the driving impetus that incited him. The Association had no inkling he was planning to disappear into obscurity while in China, hoping never to be found by them or by any government agency.

Andre could hear the seaman in the adjacent aisle. Thank goodness the aisles were dark. He knew he could not kill the seaman, as that would necessitate an investigation. He had to think fast. He quickly removed his suspenders from his trousers, stretched the elastic straps across the aisle, about four inches up from the floor, and fastened the clips into the bark of the timbers at each side of the aisle. Hopefully, the taut suspenders would act as a trip wire. He then moved into the corridor, drew his gun from its holster inside his coat and waited.

The seaman approached each aisle with caution. He had one more aisle to check and he was beginning to think one of the many rats in the cargo hold made the noise. His vigilance became more relaxed as he walked down the last aisle toward the opened end at the corridor. He holstered his gun, believing there was no reason for concern when he tripped on the taut suspenders, falling headlong into the corridor with arms outstretched and face down.

    Like a cat pouncing on its prey, Andre struck the seaman on the head with the butt of his revolver knocking him out. He bent low over the figure for a moment making certain he had not killed him and wanting to retrieve his suspenders, but they were not at the seaman's ankles. With sweat streaming into his eyes, blurring his vision, his glasses served absolutely no purpose. He couldn't see. And the shooting pain in his ankle was excruciating causing more sweat to bead on his forehead. He became emotionally out of control with fear that the seaman would awake before he could leave the cargo hold. The suspenders must have sprung farther down the dark aisle. Andre started crawling on his hands and knees searching for them, vigorously thrusting his hands along both sides of the aisle. With a yell, he bolted to a standing position as a huge, furry rat ran from his hand up his arm. Like lightening, he used his other hand to knock the rodent from his body. Frantically, he checked to see if the rat had bitten him. He went berserk, raving like a madman, and fell to the floor, with legs sprawled. He felt no additional pain other than his ankle and assumed the rat did not bite him. He placed both hands behind him to assist in getting up when his left hand rested upon his suspenders. Tears of joy filled his eyes washing away the sweat as he hobbled to the end of the aisle; he carefully stepped over the unconscious seaman and left the cargo hold.

Riding the Tail of the Dragon

CHAPTER THIRTEEN

Each of the four diners at the captain's dinner table that evening expressed a charade of stoic indifference, while a tempest of chaotic, troublesome thoughts rambled around in their minds. Each one was embroiled with a concern which, if not properly handled, could mushroom into a problem that would expose the true identity and purpose of the voyage. Because of this introspective mood, no one wanted to breach the silence with idle chatter.

Lily sat quietly at the table and contemplated the events of the day. It had been hours since she cabled London and Paris. She had made several visits into the radio room on the pretense she was expecting two cables: one from her minister with last minute instructions for her new post in Lantau, and another from her mother's doctor with regard to her mother's impending operation. The seaman appeared to be a little agitated by her frequent visits as she was interrupting his work. His head was bent low over the radio and his eyes were fixed on tiny wires. Tools were strewn all over the desk and he explained to Lily, "Something has gone wrong with this receiver again. I keep asking for new equipment, and the captain keeps telling me to fix what we have—as if I'm some kind of a magician. I try to be careful of these little wires when I send messages so I don't know how it happened that these wires came loose. If I didn't know better, I'd think that someone had used this radio today."

With a nervous laugh, Lily offered, "Perhaps, the constant roll of the ship shakes the wires loose." The sailor raised his head from the radio and gave Lily a half-hearted smile and wondered how someone could be so ignorant. Lily's eyes scanned the equipment and the tools and with a whimsical tone in her voice said, "I know nothing of electrical equipment, but I do agree with you that this stuff looks very old." The seaman assured her that he would immediately give the cables to her once they were received.

Lily pushed the peas around on her plate while she quietly issued a prayer that the seaman could repair the receiver quickly. The suspense of not knowing the profiles on Andre and Seth was eating

Jeannine Dahlberg

away at her nerves. If there were one emotion that would excite Lily, it was the fear of not knowing all the details in an operation.

With a ravenous appetite, Seth devoured the first meal his stomach could tolerate without his becoming nauseous. He enjoyed the peaceful atmosphere, but wondered why Lily was quiet—she was out of character.

Andre sat directly across the table, wincing frequently as if in pain, which Seth found disconcerting. He hesitated to speak as he did not want to break the silence and he definitely did not want to become involved in an in-depth conversation with Andre. But a moment of compassion swept over him and upon impulse and before he realized what he was saying, he asked Andre if he were feeling okay. With an insidious glance, Andre flashed his tiny, beady eyes, glared steadily at him and mumbled very low, "Young man, my health is not your concern." The answer was almost inaudible. Seth felt extremely uncomfortable, wished he had never asked the question and vowed never again, under any circumstances, would he initiate a conversation with Andre. Seth thought the Captain and Lily probably did not pay attention to the brief conversation as neither one looked up to comment.

Andre could feel his ankle throbbing. The ship's doctor had assured him his ankle was not broken, but said it was badly sprained, and dispensed a few pills with the caveat that he stay off his leg. A few words were exchanged about how the accident happened, which account was totally fabricated. During the brief discourse, Andre was able to ascertain that this seaman was a very educated man with an extensive medical vocabulary. In no way did he resemble an ordinary ship's doc aboard a tramp steamer, who at best is a seaman with a little knowledge of first aid. Andre's profession mandates that he remember peoples' faces and he had an uneasy feeling he had met this doctor somewhere long ago. The jagged scar on the doc's forehead, which extended into his hairline, was enough to jolt his memory, but the circumstances eluded him. Andre noted the doctor's general persona was cold—extremely impersonal and indifferent—without an ounce of compassion. Andre dwelt upon jogging his memory throughout the course of the dinner and did not notice that no one at the table talked.

Andre was the first to excuse himself from the table. He retired to his stateroom where he spent the rest of the evening with his leg elevated on pillows. He felt the medication he took for pain dulled his senses and he did not like the sensation. He was certain he had seen the doctor before or had been introduced to him and it greatly bothered him that he could not remember the circumstance. He closed his eyes hoping to escape from the pain when a scene flashed through his mind triggering a similar circumstance. As quickly as he imagined the doctor's face, his memory failed him and he was once again bewildered as to where he had met the doctor. His cabin room appeared to circle and dance around leaving him with a feeling of dizziness. He lapsed into a half sleep, but was conscious of a sharp pain he felt in his stomach. He focused on the pain for a moment, then rationalized the pain was probably a reaction to the excitement he experienced in the cargo hold. His nerves had been shattered for some time, playing tricks with him for the last several months in anticipation of the gold movement. He tried to calm himself with pleasant thoughts that this operation would be his last. More sharp pains passed through his stomach and he knew he would have to see the doc once again for medicine to relieve the discomfort. He would tend to that first thing in the morning.

Jeannine Dahlberg

CHAPTER FOURTEEN

A seaman's life aboard a tramp steamer can be quite hectic. There is always more than enough work for everyone. If the vessel is to clear expenses to make even the slightest profit, necessity dictates that the captain run a tight ship and the *Ladybug* was no exception. It always sailed with a minimum crew.

Captain Oscarson was a tough taskmaster who expected each seaman to perform his duties swiftly and professionally, and he had no patience with anyone who did not rise to his expectations. He developed a fine reputation for his astute business acumen and was highly respected by other sea captains. His reputation preceded him in many seaports around the world with seamen eager to sign on his ship. He exacted discipline and rewarded each seaman with a bonus after completion of the voyage according to his performance.

The war years took their toll on cargo ships, as the invading country confiscated many to serve as demanded. Because Sweden was neutral during the War, Captain Oscarson's cargo ship could sail certain sea lanes, but with great precautions. His sympathies were with the Western Allies and more than once he put the *Ladybug* and it's crew in grave jeopardy to assist them.

Shortly after the end of the War, he was able to add another vessel under his ownership, which encouraged him to develop a fleet of ships that would carry a variety of cargo to all parts of the world.

Captain Oscarson considered the trip to Macau to be his most lucrative voyage. The cargo hold bulged with expensive elm timbers and the most exciting element of this voyage was the gold bullion hidden in a few large timbers. The captain had been approached by authorities from Britain, France and the United States to assist in the capture of gold smugglers who were operating out of Macau and Hong Kong. They assured him his cooperation would be well rewarded. They explained there would be little risk involved while at sea as they would place agents aboard the ship to handle any problems, which may arise.

Captain Oscarson had sailed the *Ladybug* into the twenty-mile wide estuary of the Pearl River once before when making a short delivery with cargo from Hong Kong to Macau. He felt comfortable with sailing the river again. He was familiar with Macau's status during the War having read in the papers many accounts of refugees from the war zones safely escaping to the island. He recalled that Japan recognized Portugal's neutrality; and since Portugal considered Macau an integral part of Portugal, as opposed to being a colony, Japan did not press to capture the escapees.

Macau has always had a nefarious reputation for trafficking in gold, and the investigating authorities had informed Captain Oscarson that Portugal failed to sign the 1946 Bretton Woods Agreement forbidding the importation of gold for private purposes. They explained that gold is smuggled in and out of Macau by many ways: carried out in hollow bamboo, hammered into thin plates and worn as belts, swallowed by cows, bulk bullion by junk, etc., but this is the first time to their knowledge a shipment of this magnitude had been attempted in elm timbers. They further enlightened the captain with a background of how a transaction takes place and said that a fortune in gold bullion passes through Macau yearly. It comes openly and legally from all parts of the world through Hong Kong. Since Portugal does not belong to the International Monetary Fund and is not subject to the Fund's regulations on the import/export of gold, what happens to the bullion afterwards is private and presumably illegal. Evidence supports the conviction that the bullion is melted down on the premises to gold bars, which are then smuggled to illicit gold buyers in South East Asia, India and Latin America.

This shipment was Nazi gold, which had been looted from occupied war-torn countries, traced through Switzerland and Holland and transferred to the dock at Le Havre where the gold was concealed in timbers. They fervently cautioned the captain as to the danger involved, their expectations of his role in this assignment and emphasized the stringent rules for safety and secrecy. With a strong caveat, they declared Lily was to be treated like a passenger and the three agents—one who would double as the ship's doctor—would mingle and work with the other seamen. Captain Oscarson agreed to their demands.

Money was definitely the impetus, which urged Captain Oscarson to accept this assignment. He wanted to expand his small company and this would provide the means to add another ship to his fleet. If there would be any danger involved, he figured he had proved himself quite capable during the War and could handle any given situation on the sea.

*****

The following days were uneventful for Seth and he totally enjoyed the quiet time.

One day blended into the next and the storms that had ravaged the sea for two days cleared the air leaving a gentle breeze and a gentle roll to the ship. By choice he managed to keep pretty much to himself. He borrowed a book from the captain's spate of books, which mostly contained classic novels along with study books on navigation, astronomy, geography and political science. Seth selected "The Count of Monte Cristo" and every afternoon he would perch on top of a high storage chest at the bow of the ship and read. The captain's small classic library opened a new dimension to the captain's character, which explained his great knowledge of a wide variety of subjects. He had held only brief conversations with the captain, at which time the captain showed forth a mild manner and Seth believed his bellicose disposition was a defense in handling his crew.

Seth also used this time to contemplate his circumstances. It was easy for him to drift into a peaceful meditative mode with the gentle sea breeze fanning his body and the hot afternoon sun tanning his skin. For the last couple of days he had seen an albatross circling high in the bright blue sky and thought how wonderful it would be to soar to great heights with a feeling of freedom and confidence. What a beautiful, majestic bird—an omen of good fortune for seafaring wanderers. He realized his penchant for daydreaming, however, and would not let himself become too lackadaisical in thought—dream the afternoon away and become oblivious to his surroundings. He realized the necessity to be alert.

He tried to analyze each person aboard the ship. He observed the rigors of the deckhands as they carried out their duties, and he appreciated even more his desire to become a successful architect.

He observed the seasoned seamen did not embrace the friendship of the three new crew members, and the captain reprimanded his first mate often for his neglect of training these men. After studying these three men for a few days, Seth believed they were not cut out to be seamen. They showed no real interest in their duties and were

Riding the Tail of the Dragon

nonchalant about their training. It was quite obvious the first mate was disgusted with the three. Seth recalled an earlier conversation with the captain where he explained good men are hard to find and these three certainly enforced his thought. He made a bet with himself that the captain would not enlist these three men for another voyage.

Seth also found it interesting that only the three new crewmen approached him in conversation while he sat on his perch. All three appeared to be more educated than the other deckhands and each one took a special interest in his background—where he was from, where he was going and why, what were his interests. They asked a whole gamut of questions. Seth continued to give guarded answers, but was not apprehensive with their curiosity and took it for friendliness. He observed it was only these three who alternated keeping watch in the cargo hold, and thought it strange that it was necessary to have a man stationed in the hold during the voyage, but dismissed the thought as his ignorance in the transportation of cargo. He also learned that of these three the man named Pete was appointed the ship's doctor, since he had knowledge of medicine.

Seth enjoyed his conversations with Pete, who was a Frenchman. His first thought was to question Pete about Paris, in particular the Orleans Orphanage, but withheld any questions for fear of exposing his real purpose in traveling to Macau. Pete took a liking to Seth right away and would spend as much time as possible talking with him. He explained Seth reminded him of his young son who had been killed during the War while helping the French Resistance. His wife and two small daughters were killed in the War by SS troops, while he managed to survive the horrors of a concentration camp. Before the War, he was a professor of biology at the university and the Germans quickly engaged him to assist the doctors with their vile experiments and torture of prisoners. Some of his stories about life in the concentration camp were beyond Seth's wildest imagination and he wished Pete would not go into the gruesome details. At one point, Pete broke down and cried, beseeching forgiveness from his Father in heaven for things he had done and seen. Seth had read many newspaper articles and magazines about the War atrocities and he had seen newsreels before the beginning of feature films in the theaters, which recorded the heinous crimes so vividly. He never thought he would meet someone who actually survived the barbaric cruelty. He felt great sorrow for Pete, but thought it best to remain quiet and listen as he knew there were no words of comfort that could reach a man so filled with remorse and bitterness. Time would possibly heal his tormented soul.

He learned from Pete that Andre sprained his ankle and came to the ship's dispensary for medication to relieve pain every morning. Andre would come on deck briefly in the late afternoon for a little exercise, and it appeared to Seth that his ankle was getting stronger while his complexion was growing more sallow with each passing day. At dinnertime, Andre would grab his stomach wincing with pain, and for the last two evenings, Andre had not bothered to come to dinner. The captain and Lily made no mention of his absence and Seth did not ask. He believed Andre to be a poor excuse for a human being and was happier at dinner not having to look across the table at him. Seth believed he was a good judge of a person's character, and at times could determine a person's interest and occupation, but Andre completely baffled him. The more he surveyed his circumstances aboard the *Ladybug* the more he realized he was getting into a far different world involving intrigue. He had so many questions with no answers: who was Lily and why was she playing a double role? who were the three new seamen who definitely were not sailors? why was the captain involved with Lily? and most importantly, who was Andre? These new concerns loomed large in his mind and were beginning to consume more of his attention.

Idle time passed slowly aboard ship for Seth. He tried to stay focused on the purpose of his voyage, trying to develop a strategy to pursue in Macau in locating Rachel, but he realized he had very little information to go on—only a short note with a postmark on the envelope indicating it was mailed from Macau years earlier. Doubts now loomed in his mind dwindling the enthusiasm of his summer adventure.

He wanted to keep a positive attitude about the investigation and remain optimistic that his search for Rachel would have a happy ending. Everything in Paris that he uncovered about her existence sharpened his euphoric feeling that he would continue to have good luck. In Paris, lady luck rode on his shoulder protecting him from making any wrong moves. With the help of newly found friends, he quickly and easily discovered the whereabouts of Rachel and her family. The investigation was fun in Paris. Now, his thoughts were tormenting him that he may become involved in a serious situation by innocently booking passage on the wrong ship. He hoped that once the ship docked in Macau, he could forget his concerns for whatever evil schemes he thought were developing aboard ship, which were not his problem, and concentrate on locating Rachel. He hoped the search would not take too long, as the loneliness of this joyless voyage enforced his desire to return to the States within the month to launch his career as an architect.

Seth mentioned the sighting of the albatross to the captain and was told they were getting close to land. The captain hoped to arrive at Colon and the port of Cristobal for passage through the Panama Canal shortly. This was good news. Seth wanted to see land again and perhaps have an opportunity to stretch his legs on good ol' terra firma. He looked forward to going through the Canal locks and considered himself lucky for the experience. After crossing through the Panama Canal, the ship would continue sailing west in the Pacific Ocean, making Hong Kong and Macau that much closer. Seth smiled and thought the albatross was, indeed, a sign of good fortune.

Jeannine Dahlberg

CHAPTER FIFTEEN

"Finally! I was beginning to think these cables would never come and now they both are transmitted on the same day," Lily said as she burst into the captain's cabin.

"Lily, close the door quickly and keep your voice down. Yeah, I, too, was beginning to think everyone had forgotten about us. We are getting close to Panama and it is my understanding we will receive further instructions at that time. Quickly, how did the messages decode?" urged the captain.

"We have nothing to worry about regarding the young man, Seth. He is who he says he is. His dad is the caretaker of a large tobacco plantation, which has storage facilities in Le Havre, Macau and Athens. He graduated from the School of Architecture and accepted a position in Wilmington, which he is supposed to start in the fall. He has no prior police records or violations of any kind. It appears he is the all American boy.

"Ah, Andre has a different story. The message from Interpol is explicit. He is ruthless, unscrupulous and violent; a man of deception and disguises. There are many ramifications in his dossier, which lead French intelligence to believe he was the dominant figure in masterminding the acquisition of Hitler's wealth. His real name is Rolf Richter; and get this," Lily emphasized, "Hitler gave him an honorary title of colonel." Lily sat quietly for a moment holding the messages in her hand and continued, "It is believed that Rolf Richter and Adolph Hitler were related." Lily's voice became high pitched as she spoke, "During the last few days of the War, he had his facial features surgically altered and changed his name to Andre Reuter. The message goes on to explain that Interpol lost track of him until recently when he was questioned by Inspector LeCleur for complicity in several recent major thefts of art objects. Someone in the Interpol office recognized him, however, as the notorious Colonel Rolf Richter. Interpol decided not to arrest him at that time, as Inspector LeCleur preferred to put Andre Reuter under surveillance hoping to catch everyone involved in these robberies. That is how the authorities discovered this gold smuggling job was going down."

Riding the Tail of the Dragon

"Lily, does all this make any sense to you? I guess I have a curious mind, but you don't have to be too smart to wonder how someone at Interpol recognized Rolf Richter when his facial features and his name had been changed."

"Well, I think we will find our answer to that question when we get to Hong Kong and talk to the general," Lily presumed.

Lily continued, "I would like to have an answer right now to something that has been bothering me for the last few days."

"What's that?" asked the captain with a puzzled look.

"Have you noticed how terribly pale and weak Andre looks. He hasn't come to dinner the last few evenings. He comes on deck in the afternoons, walks—or I should say, limps—aft to gaze at the wake of the ship, then heads for the galley where I understand he asks for hot soup, but it's the limp that bothers me most about him. If you remember, he started limping right after he returned from the cargo hold. And there's another thing that bothers me. Jake was on duty in the cargo hold at the same time Andre slipped down to the hold and Jake did not see him. Here is something else that I think is crazy. Jake tripped over a rat while investigating a noise and fell to the floor so hard he knocked himself out. Now, none of this makes any sense to me."

*****

Again, Andre awoke with severe abdominal pains. He opened his eyes, straining his vision on the dancing walls, which circled to the rhythmic motion of the ship. With one hand supporting him from his cot and the other hand pulling on the small chest of drawers nearby, he managed to stand. He steadied himself for a few minutes, waiting for his balance to adjust to his dizziness. He raised his bowed head and glared into the small mirror, which hung above the chest of drawers. A shriek of disbelief escaped from his mouth when he saw his reflection in the mirror; his features appeared to be altered again. He did not recognize the man who stared back at him. For the first time in many years, Andre was frightened. He was no stranger to witnessing death; he knew its pallor well—the man in the mirror was dying.

He was still in control of his mental faculties for which he was thankful. He knew the ship would navigate through the Panama Canal shortly and dock briefly in Panama City to take on supplies. It was crucial he meet with Len Chow and it was also crucial that he visit the ship's doctor, Pete, for more medication so he could keep this appointment. The doc mentioned the medication for his ankle may cause stomach cramps, but the pain was now intolerable.

It took quite awhile for Andre to dress as he had no control over his shaking hands and he was extremely weak. His weight had dropped drastically and his clothes now hung on him. He tried to figure out what had happened to him physically. He was strong and healthy when he boarded the ship in Le Havre. Certainly a sprained ankle would not cause him to deteriorate physically. There must be another explanation. He conjured up thoughts of his ancestry to determine if any family member had died of anything remotely similar to his symptoms, but no one came to mind.

Andre left his cabin in search of Pete, who was tending to chores on the top deck. It was a shock for everyone on board ship to look at Andre in his feeble condition. Pete led Andre to the ship's dispensary and suggested that Andre see a resident doctor in Panama City, as he had no sophisticated medical equipment on board to give Andre a physical examination. Andre and Pete discussed the possibility that the medication for his ankle was causing the excruciating pain in his stomach, although Pete said it was probably an unlucky coincidence. Andre insisted that Pete prescribe some kind of an elixir that would alleviate his agony—and the doc obliged.

Andre slowly made his way back to his cabin and threw himself on the bed. He was plagued with the thought that he had met the doctor somewhere before and struggled for some time to jolt his memory. His body trembled as the old feeling of paranoia returned. Perhaps he was overly suspicious. His enthusiastic support for Hitler's rise to power and his collaboration in many macabre covert operations during the War prompted him to have grand delusions that everyone was his enemy, and his wariness had saved his life on more than one occasion. This was a different time with different circumstances and he thought: *Okay, Rolf, grab hold of yourself and calm down. No one knows my true identity. All these stupid people think I am Andre, a harmless silk merchant.* He closed his eyes hoping for some peace from pain—and he waited, and waited, and waited…and fell asleep.

CHAPTER SIXTEEN

Seth awoke early in the morning and anticipated a great day. After so many days at sea, the thought of seeing land was exhilarating and he spent the morning hours watching the distant land grow at the horizon. The Caribbean Sea was not as rough as the Atlantic had been, for which Seth was thankful. The warm breeze stirred only small swells on the water, which attributed to the playfulness of the dolphins, which appeared to be escorting the ship.

It was mid-afternoon when the *Ladybug* pulled into Limon Bay at the port of Cristobal. Seth was surprised to see the bay crowded with vessels of various descriptions flying flags from all parts of the world anchored and waiting to enter the channel. He knew that traversing the canal would be the highlight of this voyage.

Captain Oscarson was quite busy at the helm negotiating the *Ladybug's* path through the anchored vessels. It was necessary to establish a proper positioning for sequential ship entry into the channel. There was always a backlog of ships awaiting transit at the terminals and Captain Oscarson expected to wait for quite a few hours.

When the ship settled into its appointed location, Captain Oscarson approached Seth with a big grin.

"You are about to see a magnificent, brilliant engineering accomplishment; built and maintained by the United States...you know?" The captain continued in a pundit style, "It was a venture of such magnitude that no one thought it could be done. The French tried to build it and failed. It took the ingenuity, the engineering skills and the perseverance of the United States to get the job done. The cost was extremely high, though, in both money and lives. The channel cuts the Isthmus of Panama, and once we enter the canal, we will zigzag our way through three lakes...all man made and necessary in providing the vital sources of water for maintaining the ship channel over the continental divide. The flow of the water is regulated so that huge vessels can be lifted and lowered within the massive locks...and there are three sets of locks. Each lock chamber is one thousand feet long and one hundred ten feet wide. You can see that this makes it extremely important for a captain to know the

Jeannine Dahlberg

dimensions of his ship. If his vessel is too wide, it will not be able to go through the canal. It will take us about eight hours to go the fifty miles to Panama City. By using the canal, we have avoided the long voyage around Cape Horn at the tip of South America. What a marvelous legacy the United States has given the world."

Seth interrupted, "I remember reading about the construction of the Panama Canal in school and have been looking forward to seeing it first hand."

"Well then, when we are notified we are next in line to move into the channel, I'll send someone to your cabin to wake you," offered the captain, "because you will probably be sound asleep."

"I'd appreciate it, even if it is early in the morning," Seth said.

Seth watched the captain walk away with the stride of a proud man. His whole demeanor denoted self-confidence, which enabled him to control dual personalities. He could maintain a certain gentle decorum at the dinner table, where lively conversations exploded into fascinating stories on a variety of subjects; and when administering to his duties as captain of the vessel and directing his crew, he favored a bellicose disposition. Seth began to admire the man who had contrasting personalities and he admired both…the demanding, capable captain and the gentle, knowledgeable teacher. Seth knew he could find no better mentor.

*****

There was a knock at the door and Seth opened his eyes to see a glimmer of light shinning through the porthole. Pete called to him that the ship was starting its approach into the channel. Seth dressed quickly and ran down the corridor to ascend the ladder to the top deck. He burst into the open air to see the sun rise in a spectacular huge red ball. The view of the canal with the sun casting a stream of light illuminating the American flag flying over the Panama Canal Zone filled him with excitement. A feeling of pride in being an American swept over him as he gazed at the flag. He could have jumped with joy.

A highly trained pilot had already boarded the ship to guide its way through the canal. Seth sat and watched from his perch atop a high storage chest at the bow of the ship, which he now considered his special hangout, and was held captive by the special maneuvering of the ship as it was lifted and lowered through the lock chambers.

The *Ladybug* moved through the locks under its own power, but electric towing locomotives called mules ran along the top of the lock walls while harbor tugs nudged the *Ladybug* in and out of the gates of the chambers. It was late afternoon when the ship settled into the Gulf of Panama at the Port of Panama City.

*****

Captain Oscarson stood at the ship's railing watching the three passengers leave the ship to go ashore. He had no doubt that Seth would enjoy taking in some of the sights in Panama City—tourist style. Lily went ashore to send a cable to Interpol regarding the latest developments of Andre's deteriorating health and seeking further instructions…and most importantly to keep an eye on Andre. A pang of sympathy struck the captain as he looked at Andre who was a pathetic sight to behold. He knew Andre was still a dangerous man to be reckoned with, but his strength and stamina were no longer evident.

Captain Oscarson held a brief conversation with Andre before he left the ship. At the doc's urging, he advised Andre to seek a medical doctor or visit a hospital while on shore to ask for an antidote that would alleviate his pain until he could get further assistance when the ship docked in Macau. He apologized to Andre for the lack of proper medical attention available on the *Ladybug*, but insisted the ship's doctor was doing everything he could considering his limited medical knowledge. Andre acknowledged the captain's concern and said he intended to take his advice after he had met with an important silk merchant.

Andre located the small cafe where the prearranged meeting with Len Chow was to take place. Fortunately, the cafe was close to the wharf. Andre's glasses steamed with perspiration and he felt himself reeling with dizziness as he entered the small cafe. Booths were lined against the walls. He fell into one, lunged over as if in great pain, then rested against the high back of the bench and waited for Len Chow.

Lily followed Andre at a respectable distance and waited a few minutes before she entered. She decided to be quite obvious about her entrance, hoping that Andre would see her. She raised her voice to ask the waiter where the cable office was and then jokingly questioned the quality of the food. Andre turned to see Lily. She glanced at him as if surprised to see him. They briefly exchanged pleasantries and then she sat in the booth behind his where she could see the patrons who entered. Lily doubted that Andre would even remember seeing her for he appeared delirious. She began to worry what would happen if their only suspect in this gold smuggling venture would become too ill to handle the operation to conclusion.

It was after six o'clock before the cafe started to fill with merchant seamen, sailors and a few tourists. Another hour passed before Len Chow entered the cafe. He stood at the entrance for some time before he realized the old man doubled over in the booth was Andre. As he approached Andre's booth, Lily fumbled in her purse so as not to show her face. Len Chow quickly slid into the booth opposite Andre. Lily pressed hard against the tall back of her bench straining to hear their conversation. They spoke in French...which was no problem for Lily. The meeting lasted only fifteen minutes. Andre was the first to leave and Lily wondered if he would be able to walk the short distance to the wharf to board the ship.

Lily thought it best to sit at the table for a little while longer, giving Andre the opportunity to return to the ship. Andre's Chinese companion did not appear to be in a hurry to leave the cafe either. Several merchant seamen called a greeting to him in French as if he were more than an acquaintance, but none stopped to talk. Lily finished her drink and was ready to leave when she noticed another Chinese man enter the cafe and quickly walk to Len Chow's booth. Both exchanged greetings in French and then switched to another language. Mandarin Chinese was no problem for Lily.

CHAPTER SEVENTEEN

It was late at night when Lily returned to the ship. She wasn't about to wait until morning to talk to Captain Oscarson. Her adrenaline was pumping through her body and she felt she would explode with the information she had overheard in the cafe if she did not unload it immediately. She knocked on the captain's door.

"Who is it?" called the captain.

"It's me, Lily, let me in," she responded in an audible whisper.

The captain opened the door and with a gaping yawn murmured, "Can't this wait until morning?"

"Absolutely not! You'll never believe what I overheard tonight." Lily closed the door behind her while the captain poured two vodkas. Lily refused the drink stating she had already had her quota of liquor for the night and began to tell the story.

"I followed Andre to a little cafe; and as it turned out, my knowledge of French and Mandarin came in handy. The first meeting between Andre and Len Chow concerned the cargo of gold in the timbers and the role Andre is to play regarding its transfer in Macau. Len Chow told Andre he was sailing to Macau immediately to await the arrival of the *Ladybug* and he would contact him with further instructions when the ship docked. I am certain that if Andre had been in complete control of his mental faculties, he would have questioned Len Chow for more details right then, because I thought Len Chow was rather vague in his disclosure. I didn't understand at first why Len Chow didn't disclose all the details of the operation.

"It was a short meeting, but at least now I have the name of the Chinese operative in charge and he will be in Macau when we arrive. I will cable Interpol tomorrow with a full description of him. Be sure to detain your radio man so I can transmit the message."

Captain Oscarson interrupted, "What do you mean, the first meeting? Did Andre meet with someone else?"

"No, Len Chow did…and this is where the story gets interesting," Lily said excitedly. "After Andre left, I decided to hang around a little while longer and I'm glad I did. A very old, well-dressed, distinguished looking Chinese man entered the cafe and sat down to talk with Len Chow. I believe he is the brains behind this whole gold smuggling operation. Not once did Len Chow mention his name, but I will never forget what he looks like. The old man told Len Chow to get rid of Andre as soon as he arrives in Macau. He said Andre had served his purpose and it was time for him to be removed from the Association. Len Chow told the old man to consider the job done."

Captain Oscarson remarked, "Andre may not live to see Macau if he doesn't get better soon. He told me he was going to see a doctor while on shore...well, so much for getting proper medication. Our doctor will have to do whatever he can for him. We certainly can't intervene and tell Andre that he is going to be killed in Macau. That will blow your cover and the whole plan. What an evil web of intrigue we mortals weave."

*****

Giant waves tossed the *Ladybug* about the ocean as if it were a cork. Captain Oscarson had been notified before leaving Panama City that a tropical storm was approaching and that it would be best if the ship stayed anchored in the bay until the storm passed. He was assured that the winds did not have the force of a monsoon, but was a fast moving storm, which is quite common in the Pacific in August. He had been able to adhere to the schedule while crossing the Atlantic because the weather had been perfect for excellent sailing conditions, and it was extremely important the ship arrive in Hong Kong on the appointed date. He considered the risk and decided to set sail for Hong Kong, hoping to outrun the storm. The idea was good, but the plan did not work. Everything was battened down and the passengers, including the seamen who were not required to be on deck, were cautioned to stay below deck. The *Ladybug* managed to circumvent the full force of the tropical storm, but its effect was devastating to the morale of all aboard ship.

Seth felt he qualified as an "ol' salt" after the storm rolled past because he did not feel the discomfort of a queasy stomach, and he chuckled to himself when he found out that some of the seamen had become seasick. Lily was not as lucky. She came to the captain's table for dinner, but could not tolerate looking at the deliciously prepared food on the table and instead requested a dry turkey sandwich on plain bread.

Andre remained in his cabin and was seen only by the galley steward who delivered soup to him each day. The steward reported to the captain that Andre's condition appeared to be worsening and that, "he didn't look long for this world." Captain Oscarson asked the ship's doc to check on him.

Pete stood outside Andre's door for a while listening to him moan in great pain and a slight smile passed over his face. The ugly scar on his forehead even appeared to lighten in color and almost to disappear as Pete stood at the door of his accuser. He wanted to linger longer to relish the euphoric feeling and to hear the agonizing sounds emitted by the most vile, despicable human he had ever met. For many years, he prayed for the day when he could wreak his vengeance, and now that the day was at hand, he had ambivalent emotions ... uncontrollable anger for Andre's role in destroying his life and the lives of everyone he loved ... and he felt great jubilation that Andre's life was now completely in his hands. Pete thoroughly believed his actions served justice ... and *right* was on his side.

Pete knocked on the door and authoritatively called, "It's Pete, the doc."

Andre mustered a weak, "Enter."

Pete opened the door to see Andre stretched on the bed with one leg dangling to the floor as if he had attempted to get up. The foul odor in the room was pungent...the smell of impending death. Andre's eyes were rolled back in his head; his yellow skin hung on his bones; and he was wet with perspiration from an extremely high fever. Pete bent low over his body to look closer into his face. With a jolt, Pete raised his head as Andre opened his eyes and glared straight into his.

The shock of recognition upon Andre's face when he stared into Pete's face was worth every moment of Pete's long wait for revenge.

"It's you! Why couldn't I remember," Andre furiously said. "You were the first person I saw when I awoke from my operation. You were bending over me then exactly as you did now, and it's your ugly scar that I remember. You were the assisting physician in Munich when I had my facial features changed."

Andre recalled the whole agonizing incident. The first thing he saw when he opened his eyes after the operation was a long, ugly, jagged open wound on the doctor's forehead. The wound appeared newly sustained. To look at it while under the influence of the aftereffects of anesthesia was startling, if not nauseating. Andre tried to concentrate, but he no longer had control of his mind. The thought process was too difficult for him to figure out why the doctor was sailing on this tramp steamer.

"Oh, how quickly you forgot the circumstances which brought me to Munich. I hope you're alert enough to understand why I have killed you. I have dreamed of this day for many years and I want to savor every moment."

Andre's eyes closed.

With his left hand, Pete roughly grabbed Andre's shirt at his throat and lifted him to a sitting position in bed. "Don't pass out on me now, you sonofabitch!" With his right hand he slapped Andre hard across the face. Andre's eyes opened and Pete thought he noted a glimmer in his eyes as if pleading. Pete knew it was not for forgiveness of his sins—this man has no conscience—but rather to spare his life. With teeth clenched and eyes wide with hatred, Pete violently shook Andre to make him more alert and vigorously said, "You bloody bastard! Listen to me!" Andre's shoulders slumped, but Pete continued to hold him fast in an upright position.

"Do you think I could let scum like you live as long as there is one breath in my body? Hitler's ideology for a Third Reich, along with you and all his henchmen for a united Germany professing racist, anti-Semitic and pseudosocialistic ideas, aimed for a new type of dictatorship that would forge the nation into a single mass through permanent psychological and military mobilization. Such determination was spread by war and terror to bring a preponderance of authority and domination over the people of Europe. It was an aggressive plan. But you failed to take into consideration the determination of free men.

"Do you remember the fall of 1940, Colonel Richter? But why should you, it was an every day happening at that time in Paris. A High German diplomat was assassinated on the grounds of the university and a fellow Jewish professor at the university was accused of the murder. The SS troops under Himmler's command stormed the university faculty apartments that night under the pretext there were others on campus who were privy to the plot of the assassination, and rousted everyone out of bed, marched us all to the campus square where the SS troops proceeded to shoot randomly into the crowd. You were there that night. You looked so pompous and omnipotent

Riding the Tail of the Dragon

while your police executed a reign of terror over everyone on the campus. You didn't stop with the purge of human life, you emptied the university library of all books and set a huge bonfire on the campus for everyone for blocks around to see. The billowy clouds of smoke carried a wealth of knowledge into the air, but you were more concerned with the wealth of the fine paintings the library had acquired. The SS troops carefully removed all the expensive paintings and confiscated them for Hitler's treasure trove.

"My wife was killed that night." Pete faltered at this point and tears welled in his eyes as he tried to continue. "She died in my arms. Fortunately, my son was already with the French Resistance and not living with us at the time." Pete rambled on, "I don't know what happened to the other university professors and their families. There was such Pandemonium that night...I don't know where the SS troops took my two daughters."

Tears rolled down Pete's cheeks as he glared at Colonel Richter. "Do you hear me! Damn you!" Pete cried. "I don't know what happened to my daughters! I was never able to find out where they went or even if they survived that night. How can a father live with that for the rest of his life?" Pete sobbed and let loose of Colonel Richter. "I want you to suffer as I have suffered."

The Colonel fell back on the bed with his eyes transfixed on Pete's face. He was too weak to move or to speak. His eyes showed it all...he was dying.

Pete continued, "I was sent to Dachau because of my knowledge in biology and chemistry. You let me live to assist in what you termed, medical research. Yes, the SS referred to Dachau as the SS medical research center. I called it a sinister machine for dealing out death. During the first few years of the War, you visited Dachau quite often to see how experiments were developing with healthy prisoners being used as guinea pigs for medical teaching purposes and altitude experiments. I suppose you came to satisfy your lust for witnessing the macabre experiments. You never concerned yourself with noticing who else was in the room other than the victim. I watched the expressions on your face and became more repulsed by you as a human being. You're a monster!

"On one of your last trips to Dachau in 1945, you witnessed a scuffle between some prisoners and the SS. I watched also and got caught in the middle of the fight when I sustained this ugly gash on my forehead. There were more than seventy thousand prisoners in the camp at that time, and by some miracle I was one of a few prisoners who had been ordered to Munich to assist with the needs of the executive members of the Gestapo. That move probably saved my life. Shortly thereafter, Dachau was under siege by an epidemic of typhus, which purportedly caused fifteen thousand deaths. If you recall, Germany's troops were taking a beating and the Nazi command hierarchy was focusing on saving their own lives.

"That was about the same time you came to the hospital in Munich and asked to have your facial features altered. I wanted to plunge the surgical knife into you then, but reason suggested I wait. I knew at that time I would track you down if it were the last thing I would do in my life. After the War, I worked for Interpol in Paris with the hope of locating you through their resources."

Pete stopped at this point and raised his head as if to give thanks for a miracle. "Colonel Richter, I couldn't believe it when Inspector LeCleur pulled you into Interpol for questioning. Of course, I recognized you. I assisted in your facial operation. I just didn't know that you had changed your name. I thought, perhaps, you had surfaced only to be sentenced for your war crimes, like Himmler, Goering, Goebbels and others."

Pete laughed out loud and looked at the Colonel. "I was exhilarated to think that I would be the one who could dispense justice. And that is what I intend to do. You even helped me to kill you by constantly asking for medication for the pains in your stomach. Yes, I gave you a small dose of poison each time…a poison with symptoms similar to typhus. Brilliant retaliation! Quite apropos, don't you think? And you are extremely deserving of the exquisite torment you have received from me. I couldn't believe how simple it was. It was all so very easy. Vengeance is sweet." Pete had become like an animal that had stalked his prey and the "kill" was his. There was only one regret…the Colonel could die only once.

Colonel Richter's eyes were closed. Pete felt for a pulse, but there was none. To make certain the Colonel was dead, Pete took the pillow from behind his head and placed it over his face. He held it there for a while as if purging himself of a long-festered hatred. Pete felt his body begin to relax and the weight of his hostility toward the Colonel lifted from his soul. He felt free!

Pete immediately reported Andre's death to the captain, suggesting he may have died from a communicable disease and that it would be wise to safeguard from a possible outbreak aboard ship by disposing of the body quickly.

The captain agreed, "Yes, it's better this way."

Jeannine Dahlberg

CHAPTER EIGHTEEN

An atmosphere of gloom and despair remained for several days as though a black shroud enveloped the entire *Ladybug*. There was no one to mourn his death…no one liked him. Perhaps it was the bleak funeral service that lacked warmth, which contributed to an absence of conscious awareness. Everyone was on deck to witness the burial as Andre Reuter's body, wrapped in black weighted canvas, slid silently from the stretcher into the depth of the cold water.

Only twice before had Seth experienced the sorrow of death and the trauma of a funeral: when his grandfather, who was his fishing buddy, died leaving a bleak void in his young life; and when the respected matriarch of the Ramsey plantation, Miss Patti, died.

This experience was totally different. He stood at the railing and watched…seeing, but completely apathetic to the whole event as the black canvas bag plunged into the turbulent wake of the ship. He was indifferent and spiritless while his thoughts turned to Andre's reclusive personality. The only emotion Seth could effect for Andre was to feel sorry for this lonely, ugly man…a silk merchant.

Most of the men aboard the *Ladybug* had never witnessed a burial at sea and the lingering memory brought the morale of the men to its low ebb.

*****

Captain Oscarson entered the dining room with a broad smile on his face and sat at the head of the table. With a gleeful expression and a twinkle in his eye he announced, "My friends, this afternoon the *Ladybug* will traverse the 180th meridian, also known as the International Date Line, which arbitrarily demarcates each calendar day from the next. So, when the ship passes this imaginary line, it will be tomorrow. We will then enter into the Domain of the Golden Dragon, where, as legend has it, the mysterious world of the Orient awaits to provide adventure, excitement, treasure and possibly death to everyone on board. From ancient times, the dragon was the emblem of the Imperial family and until 1911 the dragon adorned the Chinese flag. Dragons are regarded as powers of the air and are among the deified forces of nature, and in the Far East, the dragon retains its prestige and can be a beneficent creature. The Orient holds a mysterious fascination, my friends, and who knows what lies ahead."

Seth was hoping for a little excitement aboard ship to quell the previous mundane days and the depressing memory of the burial at sea. He was quick to say, "A college friend of mine served in the navy during the War and told me about some of the initiation rituals marking passages over significant boundaries."

The captain recalled, "The ceremonies are ancient and their derivation is lost, but my ancestors, the Vikings, can lay claim to perpetuating this maritime tradition among seafarers of the world, passing it on to the Anglo-Saxons and the Normans." The captain paused and with reverence said, "The sea keeps many secrets and its mystery is respected by all seafarers who want to appease Neptune, the mythological god of the seas. And the Vikings included Oden, their god of war, for protection."

The captain continued, "In early times, the ceremonies were quite boisterous and rough. The initiating ritual was conducted on the sailors who were on their first cruise and traversing one of the significant boundaries; such as the equator, the 180th meridian, the 30th parallel or the Straits of Gibraltar. The ceremony was contrived to test the crew to determine whether or not they could endure the hardships of life at sea. The ceremony is quite different today…it's primarily a crew's party."

Seth asked, "Will there be a ceremony of some sort this afternoon?"

"I definitely think we have to uphold tradition and we have three first-time sailors on board," the captain answered. "We'll go a little easy on them and just give them a good wetting down. These three new men who boarded at Le Havre have not proved to be sea-worthy sailors, but I think they should experience a little piece of the ritual and have something to remember from their first cruise across the 180th meridian. Our ship's doc, Pete, is one of the three men and I think the exercise will help alleviate his depression for the death of his patient, Andre. What do you think, Lily?"

"I'm looking forward to it." Lily said enthusiastically. "I do have certain reservations, however. Will Seth and I get a good wetting down, also?"

Jeannine Dahlberg

The captain chuckled, "No, I will present each of you with a card. I have the cards in my pocket in anticipation of the event. The card reads, 'Domain of the Golden Dragon, Ruler of the 180th meridian: To all sailors, wherever ye be and to all mermaids, flying dragons, spirits of the deep, devil chasers and all other living creatures of the seas; know ye that on this day in latitude 31 degrees, longitude 180th West within the limits of my august dwelling on board the *Ladybug*, the said vessel, officers and crew have inspected and passed (your name will be inserted here) and have found you sane and worthy of the mysteries of the far east.'" The captain added, "Upon crossing the International Date Line and the presentation of this card, you will be symbolically transformed from a novice to a worthy seafarer."

The captain called his first mate into the dining room and asked that he prepare for the ceremony. The first mate responded with a broad grin and reported, "This will be well taken by the men, sir. They need a little diversion to bolster their spirits. Morale has been pretty low. I know the crew will enjoy turning the hoses on these three new men who they feel haven't carried their share of the work."

"I don't want the crew to blast the three men off the deck into the sea with the water hoses," the captain emphatically cautioned. "I will expect you to carefully monitor their fun with these men."

Seth left the dining room immediately after lunch to assume his choice seat atop the storage chest at the bow of the ship. He would be in a good position to watch the crew perform the initiating ceremony on the three new seamen.

The captain and Lily remained in the dining room and quietly discussed the situation at hand. The three novice seamen were the secret service men who reported to Lily. She knew the three were not pulling their weight with the workload and did, in fact, appear lackadaisical during the voyage. She rationalized that a good wetting with a water hose would bring some humor into the banal lifestyle of the crew even if it were at the expense of her men. Of the three, Pete was the only one who was actively performing his duty as a doctor and administering to the needs of the crew and passengers aboard ship.

"It won't be long now, Lily, before we pull into Victoria Harbor. If we have no more storms and the gods are with us, we will arrive at the appointed time. This has been a long voyage and I am most anxious to be rid of the cargo. Macau is only a short distance from Hong Kong...up the western side of the Pearl River Estuary...and there the timbers will be unloaded. I will be happy when this voyage is over."

Lily agreed. "My part in this whole operation will begin when I set foot on the island of Lantau. I, too, am anxious to have this operation behind me. The general and I will have much to discuss in order to bring a workable, safe plan to fruition. There will be many lives at stake."

Jeannine Dahlberg

CHAPTER NINETEEN

It was evening when the *Ladybug* entered the bustling harbor. A million lights from the island of Hong Kong and from Kowloon Peninsula across the bay on Mainland China sparkled in the twilight, and many lights appeared to bounce reminding Seth of fireflies dancing in the bogs of the tidewater area in Virginia. At closer scrutiny, he noticed the bouncing lights came from paper lanterns suspended from bamboo poles. He marveled with curiosity at the picturesque scene before him and recalled what his dad had said to him the last time they had talked on the phone. The idea was impulsive and he thought to himself, *the orient holds a mystical fascination for me, also.*

"Hong Kong! The queen of the orient," shouted the captain to both Lily and Seth as they stood together at the railing of the ship, while crewmen scurried on deck to prepare for anchoring the *Ladybug* in Victoria Harbor. Boats of all descriptions were everywhere and merchants on slow, unwieldy Chinese junks and smaller sampans swarmed around the larger vessels seeking to sell their trinkets and goods to any seaman eager to purchase a remembrance from the Orient.

The captain pointed to the United States aircraft carrier, *Puget Sound*, which was anchored in the bay and informed Seth that the carrier had been used during the War to transport Japanese prisoners. Seth noticed the ship rode the swells in the bay with no disturbance from the smaller boats and surmised that for security purposes the junks and sampans were not allowed to circle the aircraft carrier.

The activity in the harbor and at the wharf reminded Seth of bees swarming around their nests, electrifying the atmosphere with a charge of excitement…the likes of which he had never experienced. A short distance inland, Victoria Peak loomed majestically above Hong Kong, commanding a view of the city and harbor. He noticed the people on the dock pushing and shoving one another as if in a great hurry to go somewhere.

Lily called Seth's attention to the little boys who wore nothing at all, while the women and men were dressed similarly in dark loose fitting trousers and loose fitting jackets. Because of the warm weather some rickshaw coolies wore only a loincloth and a pair of straw sandals on their feet, while others rolled up the long trousers above the knee.

The captain listened to Seth and Lily talk and then commented, "The Chinese people are an enterprising race of people...creative, artistic and inventive. We, sailors, can be thankful for one of their inventions: the use of the mariner's compass can be credited to the Chinese voyagers, who in the late fifteenth century sailed their junks to distant ports. They were great sailors at that time and Marco Polo told of Chinese ships sailing to the southern part of Africa. It is believed the Arabs borrowed the mariner's compass from them and passed it along to seafarers on the Red Sea and the Mediterranean. Their culture is very old and interesting."

A mild breeze swept across the harbor carrying a pungent odor and Seth wrinkled his nose and said, "Wow! Where did that rank smell come from?"

The captain was quick to respond, "My boy, we are in fragrant harbor, which is a friendly name for Victoria Harbor. The Chinese discard garbage, waste and whatever personal effects they no longer need into the water. The boat people live on the water all their lives...some never venturing too far from their junks, if ever."

"If it's all right with you, captain, I'd like to look around Hong Kong tomorrow if I may?" Seth asked.

"Certainly, I think it's important that you see how the other half of the world lives. I want you to use good common sense and be extremely cautious, though, and be sure to stay out of the alleys. Your destination is Macau, and as I said earlier in the voyage, I want all my passengers to arrive at their destinations safely." The captain's thoughts quickly turned to Andre and his horrible death and he quickly added, "Of course, there are extenuating circumstances such as sickness and/or death which are beyond my control, but I plan to watch you and Lily very closely. Which brings me to mention to both of you, I plan to stay anchored in Hong Kong for one day and will leave for Macau day after tomorrow. Lily, I understand you have made arrangements by cable to Lantau for someone to pick you up in the morning, which eases my concern for your safety, and so, I plan to stay aboard ship all day tomorrow."

Jeannine Dahlberg

The captain pointed his finger and added, "If you look carefully in that direction, you can make out the island of Lantau. It's just a short distance."

Lily looked in the direction where the captain pointed and nodded, then she bid good night to the two on deck and retired to her stateroom to prepare for the morning's trip to Lantau.

The quick flow of adrenaline pumped through her veins as she opened her luggage to pack her clothes. In retrospect, she felt the crossing had gone rather smoothly. It was to her advantage that Andre had died…and, she knew the name and the description of the man who was to take his place and she also knew the description of the man who she surmised was the head of the whole operation. She thought, *so far, so good.* She was consumed briefly with anxiety for the impending meeting with the general on Lantau, wondering if their personalities and ideas would be a good blend for cooperative teamwork.

Before retiring for the evening, Lily went to the cargo hold for a short pre-arranged meeting with her cohorts who were to assist with the capture of the smugglers in Macau. The three listened attentively as she outlined her expectations for the forthcoming operation. After the briefing, each one expressed his disdain for the rather harsh hazing they received from the "old" sailors as they were doused excessively with forceful water from the hoses.

Lily suggested, "Things could get pretty messy when we get to Macau and let's hope your getting a little wet will be the worst of it."

*****

It was early in the morning when Seth went into the dining room for breakfast. The smell of bacon frying and coffee brewing whetted his appetite for a hearty meal, which he hoped, would sustain him for the whole day. He planned not to eat lunch on shore as he wanted to spend the day touring Hong Kong and Kowloon, but his priority for the day was to place a call to the States to his dad. He was surprised to learn from the cook that Lily had already eaten and was on deck awaiting her transportation to Lantau. He ate quickly hoping to catch Lily before she left the ship.

Seth arrived on deck in time to hear the captain shouting orders to a few deckhands to secure the craft starboard while Lily descended a rope ladder. The men assisted in lowering her two small pieces of luggage, which Seth thought could not possibly contain her complete wardrobe for a life-long stay on Lantau as a missionary, but then, he thought to himself, *perhaps missionaries don't require many possessions.*

Seth leaned over the railing calling to Lily at the same time, "Have a safe trip and I wish you luck."

Lily looked up to bid good-bye, but it was the other woman in the sampan who caught his attention. She was a young woman, dressed in the typical black trousers and loose-fitting jacket with her hair plaited in a queue, which fell down her back almost to her waist…and it was blonde. She was not Chinese. She was strikingly beautiful in the morning sunlight, as she turned her head upward to see who was calling to Lily. A lingering gaze held the two transfixed for several moments until the young woman blushed and averted her eyes to talk to Lily. Seth continued to stare at the young woman, watching her graceful movements on the sampan as if she were quite accustomed to the small craft. Her lithe body moved quickly to assist Lily with her luggage. They greeted one another in French, making it extremely difficult for Seth to interpret their conversation, and he wished now more than ever he could better understand the language.

Lily's assertively forceful tone of voice was reminiscent of the late night meeting he had overheard between her and the captain. It was in striking contrast to her nervous, flighty demeanor he had come to expect. Lily's actions indicated she was not pleased with the small size of the sampan, but the young woman took her remarks in stride and started to push the craft away from the ship.

Seth leaned far over the railing, hoping Lily would look up and say something to him, which would afford him the opportunity to answer, but more importantly, he wanted to speak to the young woman…but no such luck. He watched the young woman maneuver the sampan quite capably through the crowded harbor until it pulled along side a small junk where Lily and the young woman boarded. He continued to follow the course of the junk until it merged with a sea of vessels of all sizes and shapes. His mind was filled with questions pertaining to the young woman. Why did she come to pick up Lily? Was she a missionary on Lantau? His imagination raced with fantasy, as once again he contrived a dream of how a beautiful, young woman happened upon the island of Lantau. He reprimanded himself for daydreaming again, but he knew he would think about the beautiful, young woman for a long time to come.

"Penny for your thoughts...but I think I already know what you're thinking and you're right. She is a beautiful woman," the captain said with a whimsical grin as he approached Seth at the railing.

"Yes, she is," Seth enthusiastically responded, while completely absorbed with the boat activity in the harbor.

"Don't let the blonde hair fool you. You know, the Brits returned to Hong Kong in August 1945 after the Japanese surrendered and it remains a British Colony. The War took its toll on Hong Kong, though. It crumbled under a massive invasion of Japanese troops on Christmas Day 1941 after eighteen days of fierce fighting between the Japanese and the heavily outnumbered soldiers of the Winnipeg Grenadiers of the Royal Rifles of Canada. Winston Churchill reported the Canadian government mishandled the invasion of Hong Kong and referred to it as the Hong Kong debacle and wrote it off as expendable. The British Crown colony succumbed to Japanese rule and the European survivors were herded into Fort Stanley where they sustained mercilessly harsh punishment."

After a pause of reflection, the captain continued, "The island of Macau was quite lucky during the War. Japan recognized Portugal's neutrality and Macau became a refuge for those seeking political asylum or for escapees wanting to flee the ravages of a war-torn country. They successfully ran through Japan's military gauntlet and many Europeans safely sat out the War in Macau."

The captain and Seth stood quietly at the railing for some time...both engrossed in their own thoughts when the captain broke the silence and said, "Seth, the young woman could be British."

"Maybe not," Seth countered. "She and Lily spoke to one another in French."

"That doesn't necessarily mean anything," informed the captain. "Many people know many languages. How are you at French or Chinese?" asked the captain. "Or better yet...since you're going to Macau, can you speak Portuguese?"

"I can understand French better than I can speak it, and I know nothing of Mandarin or Cantonese Chinese or any other Chinese dialect or Portuguese," answered Seth.

"You mentioned you want to call your dad. Your best chance of getting a call through quickly is from the Peninsula Hotel on Kowloon. The hotel's staff consists mostly of Brits so there will be no language barrier to overcome. I'll ask two of my men to take you ashore now, if you're ready to go, and they will return for you at six o'clock this evening."

"I'm ready," Seth replied excitedly.

The captain watched as the small dinghy moved away from the *Ladybug*, and he called to his men to return immediately. All the men had expressed their desire to go ashore, but Captain Oscarson would not allow it, suggesting, instead, they could go ashore on the return trip from Macau. He wanted a full complement of men on board while the timbers were still in the cargo hold. He wasn't going to take any chances with the ship being understaffed while sitting in the harbor with a cargo worth a king's ransom.

Jeannine Dahlberg

CHAPTER TWENTY

It was still early in the morning when Seth arrived at the dock in Kowloon. He stood for quite awhile taking in all the sights and sounds of the boat terminal where people were boarding ferryboats to transport them to Hong Kong, Macau or other nearby islands. A few children were fishing off the dock, catching only small fish, but Seth admired their enthusiasm and noted how happy they were. He thought perhaps those fish would be their evening meal.

He turned to look across the few blocks to the Peninsula Hotel when he felt something fall from the terminal roof onto his shoulder. He quickly lowered his eyes to see a huge, ugly cockroach standing unabashedly. With a nervous thrust of his hand, he brushed it to the floor and noticed many more cockroaches scurrying between the marching feet of the many travelers. No one else seemed to pay any attention, but Seth decided not to linger any longer under the terminal roof and walked briskly toward the hotel.

He had to zigzag his way along the crowded sidewalks, being jostled about by the Chinese pedestrians who invaded his space at the curb while waiting to cross the street. One elderly Chinese man nudged Seth so violently, he almost slipped from the curb into an oncoming double-decker bus, which rumbled down the street rather quickly. The man slightly bowed to Seth as if to offer an apology, which Seth acknowledged.

Seth stood for a moment on the steps of the hotel admiring the magnificently designed building, which was quite formidable, commanding a regal position near the water. He remembered that Miss Patti had traveled to the Orient before the War and specifically had mentioned the grandeur of the Peninsula Hotel in Kowloon, with its opulent lobby and its furnishings and amenities being second to none. She emphasized that it was a must for anyone of social status to book the Peninsula Hotel for at least a few nights lodging while on holiday in the Orient. She lamented it had been occupied by the Japanese soldiers for their headquarters during the duration of the War and was pleased when she read the hotel had been completely renovated and refurbished to restore it to its luxurious beauty immediately after the Japanese surrendered.

Riding the Tail of the Dragon

Seth walked to the reservation desk to ask the clerk if he could place a call to the States, giving him his dad's name and phone number in Virginia. With a heavy British accent, the clerk told Seth it would be placed in jolly good time and asked Seth to take a seat in the lobby while he expedites the call. While waiting, Seth enjoyed studying the architecturally designed lobby, and he could readily understand why it is considered a world-class hotel. He believed his summer vacation was turning out to be an extension of knowledge gained through travel, seeing in person beautifully appointed buildings in Paris and in China, which would aid him in his practice as an architect. He was eager to bring this trip to a close and start his career, as he now believed he had even more knowledge to offer his employer.

Seth had not spoken to his dad since Le Havre, even though he tried to call or send a cable from Panama City. He was never satisfied with the reason given for the disruption in service of the communication lines in the whole city. As a result, Seth sat for many hours in the Western Union office near the wharf on the advice of the repairmen that the lines would be repaired rather quickly. He was extremely disappointed he could not call his dad nor was he able to see some of the sites in Panama City as time did not permit. The captain had made it quite clear everyone was to return to the ship before midnight.

Seth started to fidget with the magazines on the table next to his chair when the desk clerk called to Seth to pick up the phone located in a small room adjoining the lobby. He jumped to his feet, ran to the room and eagerly picked up the phone.

"Dad, remember me? I'm in China!" Seth blurted happily.

"Son, it's been a long time. I was beginning to worry. Where are you? Are you okay?" BillyJoe said apprehensively.

"Dad, I'm fine. Right now, I'm calling you from the beautiful Peninsula Hotel in Kowloon. I have the day to tour Kowloon and the island of Hong Kong…and then tomorrow we sail for Macau."

"How is life on a tramp steamer? Did you get seasick?" asked BillyJoe.

"Well, if you think you can swing it financially, I would like to fly home; besides it would take too long to travel by ship as I am supposed to start my job in September. I'll tell you all about these

Jeannine Dahlberg

past few weeks aboard ship when I get home." Seth said and asked, "How is the tourist season at the plantation going this summer? I was wondering if you have managed to handle all the tours without me."

"There's no doubt that I miss you. You know I don't enjoy going up to the old mansion unless I absolutely have to…and I've come to depend upon you with the tours, so I hired the neighbor boy to help with things around here until you get home."

BillyJoe continued, "Do you have any ideas how you are going to look for Rachel in Macau?"

"Yes, I'm going to the U. S. Embassy first to see if I can get any information that may help me. If you remember, I have the postmarked card mailed by Rachel from Macau and I know her father's name. Hopefully, there will be someone who may remember General von Horstmann."

"Please be extremely careful. I understand Macau is a place where easy money consorts with lost virtue…gold smuggling, money changing, opium, gambling casinos, and the list goes on with all the vices that go along with it," BillyJoe cautioned, and added, "I'll be glad when you're home."

"Dad, don't worry about me. I'll call you again in a few days. We should know by then if there is a trail that will lead me to Rachel or if I have to give up the search." Seth injected, "Dad, do you want me to stop by the Euro-Asia Tobacco Company for any reason as long as I'll be in Macau?"

"That may be a good idea. Ask Richard to send me a copy of the last shipping and financial statements so I can verify them against our records. And ask him to call me in a couple of weeks. Son, we had better get off this phone. I'll expect to hear from you in a few days. Take care."

BillyJoe was miserably hot sitting in the kitchen and longed for the summer heat to end. He rubbed his hands through his hair by habit when distressed and poured another glass of bourbon. He wanted this whole ordeal of searching for Rachel to be over…and he wanted Seth to come home safely.

*****

During the short interim of the phone call, the lobby had filled with hotel guests eagerly awaiting tour departures. Tour guides held brightly colored umbrellas above their heads, and the lobby buzzed

Riding the Tail of the Dragon

with a conglomeration of languages as each tour guide called attention to himself to attract those guests scheduled to follow that particular guide on a specified tour. The tourists, representing many nationalities, appeared to come from every corner of the world, and judging from their clothes, Seth surmised they were all wealthy.

As Seth politely nudged his way through the narrow channel of tour groups, he noticed an elderly Chinese man at the far end of the lobby who curiously traced his movement through the crowd. At first glance, Seth recognized the man as the one who had bumped him at the curb while he waited to cross the busy intersection, but he quickly dismissed the thought and left the hotel to catch the Star Ferry, which would carry him across the harbor to Hong Kong.

Passengers aboard the ferry pushed and shoved to disembark when the boat pulled along side the pier. Seth was caught up in the frenzy, but once on the dock, he took a moment to get his bearings so he would remember where to catch the Star Ferry to return to Kowloon. There were many berthing slips on the long pier and he did not want to make a mistake and board the wrong ferry.

The excitement of being in the Orient aroused all his emotions as he tried to identify with this culture, but he knew he was a foreigner in a foreign land. For the first time in his life, he took note of his height and realized he stood taller than the pedestrians hurrying past him. He walked the long pier trying to make a mental note of the sights and sounds. His faculties and senses were sharp, picking up also the pungent odor of the harbor.

At the end of the pier, coolies stood beside their rickshaws, hoping to get a customer. All looked emaciated and Seth wondered how they could muster the strength to pull a passenger in the small covered vehicle, which was supported by long bamboo poles and two wheels. One coolie looked more destitute than the other and each eagerly solicited passersby. One of the coolies, who was younger than most, called to Seth in Pidgin English. Seth noticed his richshaw was a two-wheeled vehicle attached to a bicycle and Seth thought he must be the entrepreneur of the group. Seth smiled and after negotiating a price, decided to hire him for the day, which he deemed would be a safer way to tour the city since he was by himself.

Seth noticed the same Chinese man he had seen in Kowloon climb into a rickshaw. He paid closer attention to the distinguishing

Jeannine Dahlberg

features and dress of this man—the long, pointed goatee on his chin, the queue down his back, and a skullcap of satin on his head—and he was certain it was the same man he had seen in the Peninsula Hotel. He did not want to become paranoid, but he believed this was too much of a coincidence. He reflected upon his recent conversation with his dad and he would heed his advice to be careful.

The coolie peddled down the cobblestone street while Seth sat comfortably in the rickshaw. Seth was determined to enjoy the day, but he would remain cautious. The coolie spoke in Pidgin English, which made Seth chuckle to himself at times as the broken, abbreviated sentences did not always parse. The coolie made the ride quite interesting as he possessed a great sense of humor, which was quite evident when he called out to shopkeepers along the way. His cheerful disposition exemplified his flamboyant manner, and he ran through the busy streets as if he owned them. He was a street-wise kid who appeared to know everyone along the streets of Hong Kong. The coolie and Seth managed to communicate with one another by using a lot of finger pointing and then they both would laugh. It became quite apparent to Seth they were becoming friends. The coolie's name was Chang, but everyone called him Charlie, as the coolie explained it was a name given to him during the War by the Flying Tigers, or Fei Hu as he referred to them after the shark's teeth painted on their planes. He also explained he learned to speak "fine American" from the flyboys.

At one point along a very busy street, the coolie stopped the rickshaw suddenly; quickly hopped off his bicycle to fetch a cigar butt in the gutter which had been discarded by a pedestrian, picked it up with a broad grin and placed it between his lips as if he had found a great treasure. Seth was amused by this little episode as the coolie's expression was priceless, but it drove home the point that these coolies live a simple Spartan life.

Hong Kong was definitely a shopper's paradise. Both sides of the streets were lined with small shops selling every imaginable item—from gold, silk, cloisonné, ivory, jade, pearls, parchment paintings and furs to items from all over Asia. He enjoyed watching the shopper haggle for a fair price with the merchant, who at times became a little boisterous, but both participants seemed to enjoy the

Riding the Tail of the Dragon

fray. Seth realized now why Hong Kong was becoming a tourist Mecca.

Open food markets definitely fascinated him. Dried cuttle-fish hung in bags, pork, chicken, ducks, cat and dog meat, snakes, dried rats, grasshoppers, snipes, brown worms, silkworms, grubs and more were proudly displayed to entice the hungry shopper. The thought of eating any of these was repulsive to Seth and he was happy with his decision not to eat lunch on shore.

At times, Charlie waited patiently at a designated location while Seth took a brief tour of his own to destinations where a coolie would find it difficult to traverse the terrain. The tram ride to the top of Victoria Peak presented a spectacular view of Hong Kong below and the busy harbor. He also enjoyed a ride on a double-decker bus up the mountainside to Fort Stanley. Seth regretted the speed of these quick tours, but he was conscious of the time of day and his appointed hour to return to the *Ladybug*. He was also very much aware that at each stop, the old Chinese man sat in a rickshaw at a short distance to observe his every move.

"Do you know the old man in the rickshaw parked by the fish market down the street?" Seth asked Chang.

"Oh, yeah, boss. He very bad man. Been following us all day. I keep eye on him," Chang replied.

"Do you think you could lose him on one of the side streets and get me back to the Star Ferry as quickly as possible?" Seth's request was urgent.

Chang could feel the thrill of the chase which reminded him of old times during the War when he dodged the Japanese soldiers for a myriad of reasons all pertaining to survival.

"No worry. I number one coolie. I take good care of you, boss."

With that said, Charlie peddled a circuitous route through narrow alleys and side streets at a speed which surprised Seth. People scrambled to get out of the way. No one appeared to be disturbed by the rickshaw's flight and did, in fact, call the coolie by name and offered assistance if needed. It was a reckless ride with Seth holding fast to his seat.

The rickshaw stand at the end of the pier was only a few blocks away and the old Chinaman's rickshaw was nowhere to be seen. With a deep breath, Seth began to relax. Charlie continued to keep up a good speed and was hoping he had lost the other rickshaw. He brought his rickshaw to a halt at the stand, turned to Seth and flashed that famous grin, then gave a heave of relief. Seth reached for his money from his pocket along with a big tip and handed it to Charlie.

"Boss, you number one, too," Charlie said gratefully.

Both said good-bye and then there was a moment of silence as each stared at one another. A thought flashed through Seth's mind of how life must have been for Chang during the War, which necessitated his resourcefulness. He admired Chang for his ability to survive under difficult circumstances; and he was curious to know what role the Flying Tigers played in his youthful tactical training. Seth regretted he could not spend more time with Charlie.

Charlie's thoughts were of concern for Seth's safety and he wondered why the bad Chinaman was following him.

Suddenly, from out of nowhere a rickshaw clamored to a stop at the stand. The old Chinaman beckoned to a group of three men who had been loitering at the stand waiting for the Chinaman's return to pursue Seth.

Chang yelled pointing to his rickshaw, "In, now, we go fast down pier."

Seth reminded Chang, "But the cops. You can't take a rickshaw on the pier."

"I know, boss. Cops come, arrest me; bad men go away from cops, and you hop on Star Ferry. Number one plan—no worry—it work." Chang insisted. "Cops know me long time, everything okay," Chang added.

The rickshaw rumbled down the pier with the three men in hot pursuit until the police joined in the chase. Chang slowed down at the Star Ferry slip so Seth could jump out; and with a long leap across water Seth landed on the ferry as it was pulling away from the dock. Chang continued at great speed down the long pier with the police still chasing him. The three men fell far back as they wanted nothing to do with the police.

CHAPTER TWENTY-ONE

It was after seven o'clock in the evening when Captain Oscarson was on the bridge studying the navigational charts for tomorrow's voyage up the western side of the Pearl River Estuary to Macau. He was trying to concentrate on the charts, but his mind kept drifting to Seth and his safety in Hong Kong. He specifically asked that he return to the *Ladybug* by six o'clock. His concern for Seth's safety was satisfied when he heard his voice.

Seth approached the bridge with the stride of a determined man and a scowl on his face. Captain Oscarson had never seen Seth look so distressed and unnerved.

"Captain, I need answers to my questions, now!" Seth called in an agitated voice. He approached the captain, who was alone on the bridge, and looked him square in the eyes.

"This morning an old Chinaman tried to push me off a curb into an on-coming bus and..."

The captain quickly interrupted, "Oh, he was probably nudging you to knock the evil spirit off his back. These old Chinese are very superstitious and cling to their ancestors' beliefs. They believe the evil spirits come on them over night and they must get them off their backs as quickly as possible in the morning."

"Wrong! This old man followed me all day and was joined by three more men to kidnap me...and for what reason? I have no idea. I consider myself very lucky that I hired a sharp kid as my coolie for the day and he's the one who helped me escape."

The captain was pensive in his thoughts as he looked at Seth, trying to determine if he should divulge any portion of the impending altercation with the gold smugglers in Macau. He had hoped that Seth would not become involved, but it now appeared the smugglers were watching the ship closely while it was anchored in the harbor. If the Chinaman had been successful in kidnapping Seth, the smugglers could have held him captive and bargain for the gold for his safe return if the hoist of the timber in Macau would have failed. The captain's thoughts raced rapidly. The smugglers must think Seth is an important figure in this operation. Perhaps Andre had a reason to believe Seth was a government agent on board ship and not Lily.

Jeannine Dahlberg

Andre probably told this to Len Chow during their meeting in Panama City.

Seth continued, "I overheard a conversation between you and Lily that first night aboard ship and I decided then I did not want to know what was going on. But I feel I am involved and to the extent that my life may be in danger; so, now I want the truth. What is going on?"

The captain mumbled a few inaudible words and fumbled with the charts before him. Seth felt he was struggling for an answer.

The captain asked, "You know about the gold in the timbers we are taking to Macau?"

"Yes. And I assume Lily is not a missionary as we are led to believe," Seth quickly added.

"Come to my cabin where we can talk more freely. I don't want any of my men to hear our conversation," the captain cautioned.

As the two left the bridge, the captain called to the three new seamen who were huddled in a serious conversation at the stern of the ship. He asked them to come to his cabin immediately. Pete was the first to enter the cabin and quickly acknowledged Seth with a smile.

The captain closed his door and said to Seth, "I want you to meet three government agents who have been traveling with Lily on the *Ladybug*. The general thought it best that the three men travel as seamen and Lily travel as a missionary bound for Lantau Island in Discovery Bay. I know you have talked to them while on deck so there is no need for introductions.

"I was asked by governments of several countries to assist them in their capture of smugglers in China. My part, as explained to me, is very simple. I agreed to load the cargo of timbers, knowing some timbers are filled with gold bullion, and deliver them to Macau. It was further explained to me there would be no violence aboard my ship as the cargo would be removed at once when the ship docks and I would set sail immediately to return to Hong Kong."

The captain reminisced, "The *Ladybug* and I were involved in many dangerous escapades during the War and this one I felt would be a lark, as long as I and my crew would not be physically involved…and the governments agreed to pay me quite handsomely. The incident in Hong Kong, however, alters my plans. Seth, I don't want anything to jeopardize your safety in Macau."

Riding the Tail of the Dragon

The captain looked at the three men and addressed Pete. "I'm going to hold you responsible for Seth's safety."

Pete acknowledged with a shake of his head and a look of assurance that the order would be obeyed.

Captain Oscarson dismissed Seth with a firm handshake and a pat on his shoulder, suggesting he had nothing to worry about and advised that he gets a good night's sleep.

Seth closed the captain's cabin door with the four men hovering low over charts and diagrams on a table before them. He noticed one diagram was marked, "Macau harbor and wharf area" with red pencil lines drawn extensively on the wharf area.

The idea of getting a good night's sleep after all the exciting events he had experienced during the day was absurd. He wished the captain had divulged more of what could be expected when the ship docked in Macau. Seth felt helpless and blind-sided by not knowing more of the details. He always considered he could take good care of himself in any ugly or dangerous situation, as he had proved his strength and agility many times when fighting with some of the boys on the plantation. It was not knowing what he had to reckon with that made him anxious and pensive. He did not like the suspense. It had been quite a while since his thoughts drifted to his favorite detective Charlie Chan. The thought brought a frown to his brow and a scornful smirk to his lips. This was certainly no Charlie Chan caper. It was no longer fun to think schoolboy thoughts. This was reality.

His prayers were quite lengthy that night. He rolled in bed fighting the pillow until his thoughts turned to the beautiful woman he had seen that morning on the sampan. He wondered if their paths would ever cross again.

CHAPTER TWENTY-TWO

If first impressions mean anything, Lily was disappointed when she saw the general. From everything she had been told, she expected him to be seven feet tall...a Goliath in stature. He was described to her as being larger than life with a courageous reputation for being bold-spirited with pluck and tenacity, yet chivalrous and kind-hearted.

She stopped briefly at the entryway to the courtyard to gaze upon the general who was much shorter than she imagined and a little paunchy. He stood with his back to her and she could see he held a swagger stick in his hand, which swished back and forth on the ground while he talked to a few men.

The young woman who escorted Lily to Lantau pulled at Lily's arm to walk across the courtyard to meet the general.

The young woman interrupted the group with a happy, "Hi! I'm back."

The general turned giving a sigh of relief and with a sparkle in his eye said, "Rachel, you made good time." And with a slight continental bow to Lily said, "And you must be Lily. I'm pleased to meet you at last. I've heard only good reports of your ability to grasp the strategy required under difficult situations. I look forward to working with you."

Lily liked the general right away and couldn't imagine why she felt disappointed with his appearance. Along with all his reported qualifications, she added the word gentleman.

Lily responded, "Now that I am at your headquarters, I would prefer that you call me Sydney, which is my given name. I was getting a little weary of the loquacious, whimsical personality I had assumed aboard ship. It's nice to be myself again."

"All right," the general acknowledged. "And you may call me general, or General Von as most people here on the island do. My given name is Erik von Horstmann. And you have already met my daughter Rachel."

The general hesitated before continuing, "Sydney, if you don't mind, I have some urgent business to discuss with these men and I will join you late this afternoon...say six o'clock for a cocktail before dinner. In the meantime, I would like Rachel to show you to your room. She's a terrific hostess and tour guide of this island as she knows every inch like the back of her hand. I would like you to settle in a little bit and become acquainted with places on this island before we sit down to talk."

As the two ladies proceeded toward a small cabin-like structure among a group of larger dormitory-style buildings, Sydney's eyes moved slowly from one building to another in the small tightly fenced compound, which was built to resemble a mission.

Rachel explained, "The mission was built in 1946 with the help of the monks from Po Lin Monastery," which she pointed out was only a short distance away on the island. "Mainland China was ravaged mercilessly by the Japanese who unleashed a vengeance upon the people of China that must have been festering for many centuries. After the Japanese signed the peace treaty in August 1945, children started roaming the countryside for food and shelter. Word spread rapidly in the spring that the mission had opened its doors to orphaned children seeking refuge from their ransacked villages and they started pouring into the compound from all over China. One building after another was constructed until we now have four dormitories. At the present time, however, we have only a few children."

Sydney asked, "How long have you lived on this island?"

"We came to the Orient in August 1944, two months to the day after D-Day, June 6, 1944. I remember the date well as it was extremely important that we leave France after the Allied forces had started their big push against the Nazis. So, dad, mom and I left France with the help of the French Resistance to seek sanctuary in Macau. We moved to Lantau in the spring of 1946."

Rachel opened the door to the cabin, revealing a comfortable, but small, suite of rooms. Sydney placed her meager belongings on the floor with duplicity of thought…one of relief for having arrived at her destination, and angst for the impending overt operation, which was about to begin.

Rachel lingered outside the cabin and suggested, "Sydney, I think it would be better to take a short tour of the island right now. The sky is becoming overcast with angry-looking clouds. The last few days have been so hot and sticky, I bet we're in for some bad weather. When the southwest monsoon blows, activity in the harbor and on the

Jeannine Dahlberg

islands slows to a snail's pace and that's not going to make the general happy."

The two women walked at a quick pace, which Sydney found exhilarating. She was happy to be getting some exercise after being confined aboard ship and she liked feeling solid ground beneath her feet rather than the constant roll of the ship's deck.

Sydney questioned, "You refer to your dad as general?"

"Yes, but only when I'm outside our home. There are times when I get involved in certain operations and it is better that I call him general," Rachel answered.

"I'm surprised the general allows you to become involved in this dangerous business," Sydney responded.

"I wouldn't have it any other way. My mother was involved; and after we moved to Macau, I grew up listening to conversations at dinnertime and learning strategy procedures at an early age. Our family became a tight threesome, where out of necessity, we learned to depend on one another. War is a brutal teacher for daily survival.

"Sydney, I know you're well aware of the drug trafficking and gold smuggling in Macau and Hong Kong and I know you have been thoroughly briefed on what we will be up against in the next few days. You have heard about the ugly people. I just hope you can understand there are many fine people in China who are kind and considerate, and we have been very fortunate to work side-by-side with many who willingly put their lives at risk to rid their country of the scum who feast like vultures on their own kind.

"The double life we lead puts us in contact with people on this island who are marvelous to us. They respect us for our mission work and especially for the orphanage we maintain. The residents on the island help in every way possible…the men assist with construction of additional buildings and the women make clothes for our children. These people are all so poor, but they are willing to sacrifice and share what they have. And the monks are generous beyond belief. The little children love to see them come to the orphanage. They provide milk for our many orphaned children who grow to adults here…and one-by-one move out to pursue their place in the world. This is what makes the dark side of our life all worthwhile. We want these children to grow up in a healthy environment and to have the

Riding the Tail of the Dragon

opportunity to live in a society where the evil element has been harnessed.

"Oh, Sydney, it is so sad to be an orphan with the heavy-hearted feeling that there is no one in the whole world who cares about you. It seems that most of my life has been spent in an orphanage and I can empathize with these children. Each child has a story that brings tears to my eyes; and I feel if I can help just one child know that someone cares, then my staying here fulfills my desire to reach out to these children. Perhaps, that is why I plead with my dad to let me stay here. He would like me to return to France, as he puts it, to live a happy, normal life."

Curiosity overcame Sydney and she asked, "How did the general happen to be charged with heading the intelligence office in the Orient?"

Rachel responded, "We had been living in Macau for only a few months when he was approached by Philip Preston of British Intelligence to accept the key position. Mr. Preston explained the offices of British Intelligence and Interpol were working closely together to quell the rapid expansion of drug trafficking and gold smuggling in Hong Kong and Macau. He mentioned Inspector LeCleur, of Interpol, highly recommended the general for the position.

"Well, Sydney, you must realize, my dad was a military man all his adult life...and a high-ranking one at that. He carried responsibility and authority with the grace and ease of a bird floating on the morning breeze. After three months of solitude on Macau with nary a thing to do, he was ready to jump back into the only life he knew...the excitement and drama of strategically planning against an enemy, and this time the enemy is the Triad Society of Hong Kong.

"It was my mother's idea to build a mission on Lantau which would be cover for the general's headquarters. The idea for expanding the compound to accommodate an orphanage came quickly when my mother saw all the children coming out of the hills for refuge."

The island was beautifully verdant with pathways leading in every direction. Rachel was aware that Sydney's stride began to slow down after an hour of walking at a quick pace. The women chatted only now and then when Rachel pointed out a particular landmark or site of interest, such as the monastery and the reservoir. Sydney was quiet and conserved her breath for the long walk.

Rachel broke the silence screaming and grabbed Sydney from the path. With a look of fear in her eyes she exclaimed, "Please be careful where you walk, Sydney. Always keep your eyes on the path. There are poisonous snakes on this island including the dreaded cobra and they like to sun themselves along the narrow paths."

Sydney took a deep breath as she watched the snake slither away and said, "I guess I owe you one."

"I don't think I'll ever get used to them. Snakes unnerve me...and that big one startled me." Rachel shivered and shook off the fear.

They continued their walk in silence and circled back to the mission.

Children were laughing and playing in the courtyard when they returned. Sydney felt a pang of nostalgia, remembering the days of her youth when she was carefree with only one thought—how she could fill the day with happiness. Oh, the insouciance of youth—what a blessed time!

Sydney noticed there were more men in the compound than earlier in the day. It was almost five o'clock and she was anxious to meet with the general at six to discuss plans. As her eyes scanned the men, she tried to figure out, which one was Quan Lee, who was in charge of the Hong Kong security division. He and his men would play an important role in the capture of the gold smugglers.

The two women stopped at Sydney's cabin door. Rachel said, "I hope I didn't tire you on our long walk. Actually, there is so much more that you didn't see. Lantau is a very large and beautiful island. Well, I'm going to freshen up a little bit for dinner so I'll see you later."

"I'm looking forward to meeting your mother at dinner tonight," Sydney called.

Rachel returned to the doorway and stood even closer to Sydney as if to divulge a secret. There was a long pause. "Sydney, that will not be possible. My mother was killed shortly after we moved to Lantau. Our third dormitory was under construction with debris and building material lying all over the ground. Mother insisted the area be kept clean so snakes would not hole up close to the other dormitories where the children live and play. One little girl lost her ball in the debris and mother quickly ran to retrieve the girl and her ball. As she bent down to pick up the ball, a cobra bit her on the cheek. She died very quickly. It was after her death the general put up this tight fence around the compound to deter, to some extent, the infiltration of snakes…and as it turns out…the fence offers a safer compound for many reasons."

Jeannine Dahlberg

CHAPTER TWENTY-THREE

Sydney eagerly awaited the appointed hour for cocktails and when the clock finally chimed six, she was out the door and the first to arrive at the general's home. Introductions were made during cocktails when everyone was present. With four nationalities represented—British, German, Chinese and French—it was agreed that everyone would speak in English.

Cocktails and dinner were extremely delicious and satisfying. Sydney appreciated the chef's efforts aboard ship, but the menu was greatly limited to a few of the chef's specialties, which lost their appeal after the long, grueling voyage. During dinner, conversation was limited to mundane subjects with no one breaching the confidentiality of any plans previously discussed. After the seven course dinner had been served and everyone appeared comfortable and relaxed, the general invited the group to his office. Sydney thought to herself, *finally, we are going to get down to business.*

The general pulled out charts and maps of Macau and placed them on the table before him with absolutely no speed. His movements were slow and deliberate as if he were delaying the start of the meeting. The hour was getting late...almost ten o'clock when there was a knock at the door. Rachel opened the door and to Sydney's surprise, Captain Oscarson and Pete entered.

Pete did not wait for an introduction, but moved quickly to shake the general's hand. With a warm handclasp he said, "Inspector LeCleur has told me all about your work for the French Resistance during the late years of the War and I'm proud to shake your hand. I served under Inspector LeCleur for a few years and I know he does not bestow accolades readily."

The general, feeling a little embarrassed, acknowledged Pete's compliment and then turned to Captain Oscarson with a question. "Were you followed?"

"No, but it took quite a bit of fancy maneuvering in the harbor on a little sampan to shake them off our trail. The wind is starting to kick up and the sea is becoming quite heavy, which made it even more difficult. I hope they are wrong about a monsoon coming in. That's only going to complicate matters."

Captain Oscarson explained in great detail Seth's experience and encounter with a few members of the Chinese Triad while on shore. It was the consensus of opinion that Seth should be well guarded while in Macau and Pete stated he would be responsible for his safety. The captain stressed the necessity to protect his ship from damage during the unloading of the timbers as he wanted no trouble aboard his ship.

Captain Oscarson asked the general, "Why did you feel the need for me to be here at this meeting? I really did not want to become involved in any plans dealing with the transfer of the cargo."

Quan Lee spoke, "I am the one who asked the general that you be invited here tonight." He spoke with great passion when he continued, "My men have consulted with the feng shui master, and it is urged that we wait one day more before the ship arrives in Macau. The wind has been playing havoc with natural forces of wind and water all day and the master advises we wait for positive qi, when the zone of energy is in our favor. If we do as the master advises, it will bring good fortune. We must not ride on the tail of the wind, but wait for a balance in cosmic power. Please accept these feng shui crystals and candles and place them near a passageway aboard your ship."

Captain Oscarson was well aware of the power of feng shui. Its ancient traditions practiced for thousands of years in China exert a slavish following among the people. He feared that if he did not do as asked, there could be adverse ramifications, which would bring disaster to this whole operation and the blame would rest on his shoulders. He certainly did not want any harm to come to Quan Lee and his men. He agreed to delay sailing to Macau by one day.

The meeting lasted into the morning hours with detailed strategy being discussed. It was Quan Lee who asked that more armed men be present when the *Ladybug* docks in Macau. He explained the number of men in his division had been cut to half because of the Hong Kong flu epidemic, and he suggested he could muster a large number of mercenary soldiers, who had drifted into Hong Kong, in a few days' time.

The general was well aware of the infiltration of professional soldiers who were arriving daily from Indochina as their infamous reputation preceded them.

"You're referring to the Legionnaires, right?" asked the general.

"Yes, we could assemble a sufficient cadre of soldiers, which could be stationed at certain intervals along the road from the wharf to the warehouse where the timbers are to be delivered." Quan Lee continued, "and as we have determined, the Triad will make its move to hijack the timbers with the gold at some point along the road, while the timbers are being transported."

Captain Oscarson listened with great interest as he knew they were talking about the soldiers of the French Foreign Legion. Their reputation for heroism, as well as being uncontrollable mischievous scamps, was known world-wide.

After much deliberation, the general agreed to use the Legionnaires with a strong caveat to Quan Lee that the men were to follow his instructions explicitly.

A fierce storm raged most of the night during the meeting with no one giving it any attention. It was only when the meeting ended and each participant was to return home that the heavy rain drenching the compound into a sea of mud reminded the group that the bad weather was also an issue to be considered. They all quickly agreed the *Ladybug* was to stay anchored in the harbor until the storm subsided. This would also provide Quan Lee with more time to assemble the Legionnaires.

Sydney was the only one who stayed after the meeting ended to talk to the general. This was her first opportunity to discuss her concerns with him in private.

Sydney spared no details in telling the story of all the intrigue aboard ship involving Andre, and she described as best she knew the circumstances surrounding his horrible death. She mentioned how she had riffled through Andre's belongings in his cabin after he died and how she was unable to find anything that would incriminate his being involved in any crime. Sydney further explained that it was a stroke of luck that Pete discovered Swiss bank account numbers tattooed on his left ankle while preparing his body for burial at sea.

The general expressed how pleased he was with the discovery of the Swiss bank account numbers, and suggested that after a thorough investigation into Andre's accounts, perhaps the money could be traced to the rightful owners. He told Sydney he would cable the authorities immediately so they could recover the fortune.

Riding the Tail of the Dragon

Both the general and Sydney were startled by a loud clap of thunder, but it diverted their attention only briefly. Sydney continued her story regarding her encounter with Andre in Panama City where he met with Len Chow, and she enthusiastically reported the conversation between Len Chow and the distinguished looking Chinese man who commanded Len Chow to kill Andre upon his arrival in Macau.

The general quietly pondered this information and asked Sydney to give as detailed a description of the old Chinese man as possible. While Sydney described the Chinese man as best she could, she noticed the general's facial expressions brightened as if he knew the man she was describing. To her dismay, the general said nothing more to her and suggested she return to her room to get some sleep.

The wind caught the door as Sydney opened it to leave. She managed to jump over the many mud puddles and sprinted to her room as if she were a young gazelle prancing across the African plains.

The small suite of rooms she now occupied was certainly more comfortable than the little cabin room aboard ship with its one porthole. After undressing, she quickly crawled into bed. It had been a very long day: the arduous walk taking its toll on her physical strength and the zealous meeting emotionally draining her nerves, which were now teetering on the ragged edge. *Only a few more days and this escapade will be over* was the thought, which enabled her to persevere mentally. She relived the conversation she had with the general as she waited for sleep to overtake her. Her concern was with the general's reluctance to take her into his confidence regarding the identity of the Chinese man. She was not fully gratified with the meeting.

CHAPTER TWENTY-FOUR

All anchored ships in the harbor including the *Ladybug* rocked and rolled on windblown waves like fishing corks bobbing down a swiftly moving stream. The storm never escalated to monsoon force, but boat activity had been greatly curtailed as the rain continued to pounce the region.

Seth awoke to the patter of rain on the water, stretched vigorously, exercised for a good twenty minutes, which was his daily routine, showered and dressed for breakfast. The thought of breakfast with his dad standing at the stove preparing his favorite omelet was almost more than he could bear. He realized he was beginning to get a little homesick and his insatiable appetite for his favorite omelet would not be quenched until he returned home. The word "home" had a nice ring to it, but a dark cloud muddled these pleasant thoughts as his mind conjured up the predicament in which he was now involved.

He entered the dining room and was surprised to see the captain and Pete still lingering over coffee at the table. The captain appeared to be agitated as he spoke to Pete, and with a quick gesture to Seth, invited him to sit with them. They continued their conversation while Seth drank his coffee and listened.

In a consoling manner, Pete suggested to the captain, "The Legionnaires are already trained in warfare; they have the experience and certainly the reputation for being outstanding soldiers."

"I know all that," the captain said in an irritable tone of voice. "I just don't like the idea of so many people becoming involved at the last minute. That's when things can go wrong."

There was no conversation for a few long moments. Seth decided to jump into this little meeting to try to find out more about what action would be taken in Macau and to what extent he would be involved. He asked, "Did you say Legionnaires? Do you mean the French Foreign Legion?"

"The very same," answered the captain. "What do you know about them, Seth?"

"Well, I guess not much. What I learned was from watching a movie some years ago titled 'Beau Jest' with Gary Cooper, and the

Riding the Tail of the Dragon

Legionnaires were depicted as being a tough bunch of men who suffered brutalizing discipline under their officers."

"That's about right," assured the captain. "The Foreign Legion was born in 1831 to absorb the footloose veterans of Napoleon's old armies and the corps continues to grow today with men wishing to be soldiers of fortune. My concern is that they have unpredictable dispositions. They are renegades from countries all over the world, who pledge allegiance to the Legion and to no other country…not even to France. They are asked no questions about their past when they volunteer and many are known to be Nazis and Fascists who are eager to join to lose their identity in the corps. They are men without a country who pursue the only way of life they know—professional soldiering."

The captain mumbled inaudibly to himself for a moment and then continued, "In their defense, though, I should add…the French Foreign Legion is the most decorated corps in the world and its reputation was reaffirmed and exemplified by the Legion's performance in Indochina during the War."

The captain again became quite agitated and in a loud voice exclaimed, "I don't want these Legionnaires to seek their fortune in gold bullion by heisting the timbers they will be hired to protect from the Chinese Triad. I'm concerned they may shift their loyalty."

Pete was quick to add, "Let's not borrow trouble. Quan Lee will hire a small number of men—only enough to help out—and I'm certain he will be extremely selective. And I believe the final decision will be made by the general."

Seth saw the captain clench his teeth and almost snarled when he said, "I don't want a rogue's gallery of misfits. I have often heard them referred to as the legion of the damned."

Seth had never seen the captain so enraged and hoped to relieve this tense moment by asking, "Are we going to sail today for Macau?"

"Of course not!" blurted the captain. "Didn't you see the crystals and candles in the passageway? The feng shui master suggests we wait in the harbor until the zones of energy in wind and water comply with a positive stabilizing force, which will bring good fortune to our voyage to Macau. And I'm not about to buck superstitious nostalgia for the spiritual beliefs of ancestors that go back thousands of years.

Jeannine Dahlberg

If it's going to take feng shui to get my ship and men safely home, then I'll do whatever it takes."

The men sat quietly for some time…each embroiled in his own disquieted thoughts with only the slight tinkling of crystals in the passageway breaking the silence.

With great deliberation, Captain Oscarson began, "Seth, this morning I received a message from the general requesting your participation in going ashore to contact the rickshaw coolie, Chang, and he wants you to be accompanied by one of his men. He emphasized there should be no danger involved, as he has undercover men stationed in Hong Kong near the rickshaw stand who will protect you if the need should arise.

"Last night, I learned your young friend Chang is well-known in certain dubious societies throughout China. It appears he knows influential people of many nationalities who trade in commerce of various commodities."

Seth was a little stunned by this request and asked, "What am I to say to Chang, or Charlie, when I find him?"

"Nothing. The general's man will do all the talking. I'm not privy to the necessity for this meeting, but I understand it will take only a few minutes."

"I really didn't want to become involved in this," lamented Seth.

"Neither did I," assured the captain, "but it looks as though we are in it together."

"When do I leave?"

"The sampan should be here within the hour."

Seth left the dining room to the tinkling sound of feng shui crystals and went to his room to consider the precarious situation, which confronted him. The rhythm of raindrops upon his porthole window washed away any fear he may have had…with the slow, constant patter of the rain having a soothing effect as he pondered his predicament.

From the first night aboard ship when he overheard Lily and the captain discussing gold bullion in the timbers, he experienced an uncomfortable feeling that he may somehow get caught in the middle and need to protect himself. He tried to remain reticent and suppressed any desire to become involved; but now that he was involved, he felt his spirit had been imbued with energy created by the opportunity to have an active role in his own destiny…if, indeed, his life were to be at stake.

His personality and mental disposition would not allow a fatalistic belief…where he would be content with waiting for the impending tide of events in Macau to steer a course…one which may cause him harm. He genuinely relished the exciting idea of getting involved.

Last remnants of rainwater continued to rush off the deck as the storm rolled out of Victoria Harbor leaving the sun's rays to permeate through the dark clouds painting a magnificent rainbow over the city of Hong Kong. It was a good omen Seth thought to himself as he watched the small sampan pull along side the ship.

Jeannine Dahlberg

CHAPTER TWENTY-FIVE

A shrill, piercing noise awoke Rachel. Of all the sounds in the world, it was the irritating buzz of her alarm clock, which bristled her temperament into a sensitive mood. She only used the alarm on occasions of necessity, and it was important that she arise early in the morning.

She quickly dressed, putting on a pair of loose-fitting black trousers with the customary piece of garment hanging in front down to the ankles, like an apron, and another piece hanging behind in the same way. As she reached for her long black jacket, which reached to her knees, the wide sleeve hooked onto the pull of her dresser drawer, opening the drawer to reveal a sheathed knife. She took the knife and securely fastened it to the belt of her trousers; slipped into the jacket and glanced into the dresser mirror. A broad smile reflected her pleasure at the deceiving disguise as she tucked her long, blonde braid under the black silk cap. She had donned these garments many times, along with the sheathed knife, and felt quite comfortable.

Rachel stood for some time looking at herself in the mirror, thinking the clothing no longer helped her to look like a boy as it did a few years ago. Her body had developed into a curvaceous figure where the clothing did not hang like baggy garments. She thought to herself, *I couldn't deceive anyone now…I am a woman.* She realized her emotional disposition had changed over the past few years as she became more inclined to dwell upon romantic scenarios. There were many times when she lay in bed at night wishing her mother were still alive to answer her many questions. She never approached her dad; he was always too busy anyway with far more serious problems. He did request that she keep her distance from the men under his command, suggesting they were much older than she.

Rachel believed the only disadvantage to living on the island of Lantau was at times she felt isolated from young people her own age. She lived a cloistered life, which had never bothered her when she was younger, but she was beginning to regret she had no young friends…girls or boys. She lingered a while longer in front of the

Riding the Tail of the Dragon

mirror, checked to make certain the knife was concealed, and left her room to meet the general for breakfast.

She and the general stayed up quite late after everyone had left the meeting the night before to discuss the information Sydney had revealed about the conversation she had overheard in the cafe in Panama City. Rachel could read her father's facial expressions very well and it was quite clear he was pleased with the description Sydney had given of the distinguished looking Chinese man. She knew their paths had crossed before and the Chinese man had proved a formidable adversary. Now, the general knew for a fact who was the leader of the gold smugglers and he could adjust his strategy accordingly.

The general was already seated at the breakfast table when Rachel entered. He looked quite worried when he said, "Rachel, I want you to be extremely careful this morning. You know, you are my little girl."

"Dad, in case you haven't noticed, I am a young woman and quite capable of taking care of myself, which I have proven over the last few years."

"Yes, I realize your capabilities, but I want this job to be your last one. It's because you are a woman, and in case you haven't noticed—a very beautiful one, that I want you to return to France where you belong. Promise me you will at least consider it," the general encouraged.

"Okay, dad, I'll consider it," Rachel replied. "Just stop worrying about me."

*****

Rain and wind were no longer concerns when Rachel hopped into the sampan to execute the errand the general requested. She would travel alone until she arrived at the *Ladybug* where she would pick up a passenger who had met Chang in Hong Kong the day before and who knew what he looked like. She was familiar with Chang's many escapades during the War, as he had carved out quite a fine reputation in assisting the allies against the Japanese; however, she had never met him.

Rachel was distracted by the colorful rainbow over Hong Kong when a large wave dashed the sampan against the *Ladybug*. The impact startled her, causing her to lose her footing, and she sat down rather abruptly, vocalizing a slight groan.

The captain had joined Seth on deck to await the sampan and both looked at one another in surprise when they heard the quiet cry…it was a female voice and they were expecting the general to send one of his men.

A voice from the deck above called, "Are you okay?"

Rachel mustered a rather deep voice to respond, "Yes, of course."

She tried to hide her embarrassment as she glanced upward to see two men standing at the railing: one, was Captain Oscarson, whom she had met the night before, and the other was the young man she had noticed at the ship's railing when she picked up Lily to take her to Lantau.

Occasionally, Rachel would think about the young man. She liked that he was tall and handsome and would fantasize various vignettes, which would include him in her imaginary dreams.

Seth descended the ladder much to her chagrin. She never dreamed she would see him again and flashes of her imaginary dreams made her blush. She managed a sheepish smile to greet the young man then turned her head so he could not see that she was flustered.

Seth introduced himself, which Rachel acknowledged with a nod of her head. She felt very uncomfortable with the thoughts that were racing through her mind, said nothing, and promptly steered the sampan the short distance to Hong Kong. She could feel Seth watching her as she adeptly maneuvered the craft to the dock. It distracted her a little bit, but not enough so that Seth could notice. A warm feeling rushed through her body…something she had never experienced before…almost like their souls were communicating. The idea scared her and she dismissed the thought immediately.

It was disappointing for Seth that there was no conversation during the short ride. He had at least hoped to get her name.

After the sampan was securely tied to the dock, both headed for the rickshaw stand. Both now projected their thoughts to the serious business at hand.

The foul odor of the harbor was more than Seth could tolerate and in a protective manner he reached for Rachel's hand so they could zigzag through the crowded area faster together. His eyes scanned the faces wondering if any of the general's men would flash him a high-sign giving him a sense of security; or worse, if he would see the old Chinaman who chased him around the city. With a sigh of relief, he noticed Pete shopping at a market near the rickshaw stand.

Coolies eagerly solicited passengers, calling to everyone within earshot in various Chinese dialects. The pushing and shoving crowd appeared more intense as each pedestrian cried out to a specific coolie. Seth was experiencing morning rush hour in Hong Kong with the sights and sounds of business people hustling to their offices reminding him of New York City.

Seth and Rachel took refuge from the crowd in a small doorway of a haberdashery where Seth continued to scan the boisterous group of coolies looking for Chang.

A slight chill passed through his body when he noticed the old Chinaman talking to a small group of men by the curb of the road a short distance away. He felt fairly safe from view hiding in the doorway and thought with any luck the old Chinaman would leave.

Time passed slowly as they stood quietly, neither one breaching the silence. Both felt emotions accelerating with anxiety to find Chang, quickly. As the crowd of passengers and coolies diminished, seeking their appointed destinations, Seth saw Chang's unique bicycle rickshaw parked at the far end of the stand. Chang was slowly meandering toward his rickshaw holding a cup of tea.

The old Chinaman had walked farther down the road and Seth waited until the Chinaman no longer looked in their direction when he again reached for Rachel's hand in a gentle, supportive grasp, pulled her from the doorway and started running toward Chang's rickshaw. Chang's face brightened when he saw Seth and with a broad grin on his face called, "Hey, boss, you come back. Bad men not scare you away. I not expect to see you again."

"Charlie, I'm here at the request of the general on Lantau Island and it's a matter of urgency," reported Seth.

"Oh, boss, he very big man; he like dynamo at power plant…much force. How you come to know General Von?" Charlie asked.

"That's not important now…I want you to meet…" Seth did not have a chance to finish the sentence when Rachel grabbed Charlie by the arm and started walking away from Seth while conversing in

Chinese. He noted Charlie's facial expression changed dramatically from cheerfulness to consternation. What did she say that changed his mood so quickly, he wondered.

Gunshots rang out across the road from the rickshaw stand and Seth saw Pete running toward the three of them. With a violent gesture of his hand pointing to the wharf, Pete motioned for the three to run with him to the dock. He called, "Get to the ship!"

No one asked why…they could see from the men chasing Pete that there was trouble. Seth thought as he was running, *how could this be happening to me again. This is the second day in a row that I'm running for my life down this long wharf to get away from someone chasing me.*

Pete saw the girl's sampan and stopped running to let the three go on ahead. He would stave off anyone in pursuit of the three as they jumped into the sampan.

Seth reached for the rope to untie the craft from the wharf. His dexterity lacked swiftness as his fingers felt like all thumbs. Rachel whipped out her knife, cut the rope quickly and the sampan was free in the water. Charlie navigated the craft for the open harbor and the three breathed a sigh of relief. Seth looked back to see Pete waving them on and pointing farther down the long wharf to the activity at the rickshaw stand. The general's men, who were stationed all around the area, came running like pigs to a feeding trough and surrounded the small gang of hoodlums who Seth perceived to be members of the Chinese Triad.

CHAPTER TWENTY-SIX

After Pete safely returned to the *Ladybug,* Captain Oscarson wasted no time hoisting the anchor and setting sail for Macau. He no longer cared what the feng shui master prophesied. He no longer cared that the ship would ride the tail of the dragon. He was not going to put his men and ship in jeopardy sitting in the harbor like a wounded pigeon...vulnerable to an attack. It had quit raining hours earlier and the wind was no more than a stiff breeze. What was there to fear from feng shui...*the captain was not a superstitious man.* He surmised, the general's and Quan Lee's men were probably already in Macau, and with a scornful smirk added, along with some Legionnaires. He gave the order to his men...and the ship moved out of the harbor.

Charlie was disgruntled to think he was now involved in something where "bad men keep chasing Seth," and he did not like the idea he was sailing to Macau against feng shui. He held his bowed head with his hands and rocked it back and forth moaning, "We all in big trouble. Oh, man! We ride tail of dragon! It may be good, or...it may be bad. It depend on feng shui."

Captain Oscarson put his hand on Charlie's shoulder and tried to console him, but Charlie would not be persuaded.

Charlie raised his eyes showing a furrowed brow and cast a wise look, as if old beyond his years, alternating from the captain to Seth and then to the girl. "You think General Von powerful man. Maybe with mortals," he opined. Charlie opened his arms wide, swinging them from side to side and continued, "Feng shui control all nature and elements of whole world. General not in same class as feng shui."

In a tone of regret, the captain said, "Charlie, I'm not pleased that things have not gone according to plan. We must leave the harbor, now. The general has asked that you and Rachel sail with us to Macau."

The captain left the three standing on deck to return to the bridge to assist navigating the *Ladybug* as it proceeded slowly through the wide estuary of the Pearl River.

Jeannine Dahlberg

Seth couldn't believe what he had just heard. The girl's name is *Rachel?*

With a surprised look on his face, he asked, "You're name is Rachel?"

"Yes, my name is Rachel," she quietly replied, thinking *what is so strange about my name.*

"Is your father General Erik von Horstmann?" Seth was so energized asking the question that he exuded happiness, which caught up Rachel and Charlie in his excitement.

"Yes, he is," Rachel hurriedly acknowledged.

Seth quickly put his arms around Rachel, gave her a big hug, picked her up and swung her around, expressing great joy. It was beyond his belief that he could be so lucky. He thought, *if I'm riding the tail of the dragon, the positive forces of cosmic energy must be with me.*

Rachel and Charlie glanced at one another with eyes wide and a quizzical stare. They couldn't help being swept up in Seth's jubilation, happy to be relieved if only briefly of the fear and anxiety of their escape from Hong Kong. It was a nervous reaction that prompted a broad smile as Rachel waited to hear the reason for Seth's happiness.

Seth quieted down and was about to tell the story when Captain Oscarson interrupted the three with a call from the bridge to Charlie. Charlie flashed a look of disappointment as he wanted to hear Seth's story, but quickly obeyed the captain's command and ran to the bridge.

With a gentle touch, Seth took Rachel's hand and guided her to his favorite spot on deck—the storage chest—where for the next few hours they sat together. Seth talked incessantly, thoroughly explaining to Rachel the urgency to locate her and bring her back to Virginia.

He described the plantation as he remembered it when Miss Patti was alive and related the great stories he had been told about the "old days" when the plantation was visited by foreign dignitaries and royalty. He spoke with pride when he explained the zealous role his family rendered as caretakers responsible for managing the plantation to its greatness. He told the story with great passion, never before realizing the magnitude of its importance upon his life. He paused to consider his emotional ties to the plantation and then continued. Rachel sat quietly.

His search for Rachel in Paris was told with gusto, as his enthusiasm spilled into each episode encountered bringing him closer to her discovery. After each disclosure in the series of events, he emphasized his good fortune and remarked several times...the positive forces are with me.

He explained everything very clearly: locating a record of her birth at the hospital; finding her mother's interment records at the cemetery; talking with Mother Superior at the orphanage where she told the story of her adoption by General Erik von Horstmann; concluding with his meeting with Inspector LeCleur at Interpol.

Rachel's response was not what he had expected. She listened intently to the story, but interrupted many times with questions regarding its validity. She reflected upon her loving parents, the years of daily struggle for survival during the War at the orphanage with her mother; the sea of troubles the three of them experienced in Macau; and all the hard work involved building an orphanage and headquarters on Lantau. She always felt loved and protected even under the most dangerous circumstances. It was a tight family unit, which grew in strength and love from each perilous incident. Not once did she have any reason to believe she was adopted. She had no reason to believe his story and every reason to discredit his account of her adoption. Why should she believe a total stranger?

With that thought, Rachel asked, "Do you have anything to prove I'm Rachel Ramsey?"

That question quickly sparked Seth's memory and he hopped off the storage chest, took her hand in his and said, "Wait here. I'll be right back."

Rachel lowered her head in disbelief, asserting this was all too much excitement in one day. She anticipated the possibility of putting her life in jeopardy while talking with Chang in Hong Kong, but nothing prepared her for this emotionally traumatic story she had just heard. She didn't want to believe it.

Seth returned holding a hand-written note postmarked Macau. Rachel took the note, fondled it and lovingly looked it over while tears welled in her eyes. She remembered writing the note. It was written under difficult circumstances when she and her parents were

Jeannine Dahlberg

in hiding in Macau. She began to cry as Seth tenderly slipped his arms around her in a consoling fashion.

They sat quietly together for a long while, watching piscivorous birds overhead searching for fish in the murky water. Ubiquitous bamboo trees, the prince amongst trees in China for all its purposes, lined the banks of the river and people of all ages spread along the river's edge exerting an exercise in Tai Chi…a slow moving motion practiced for balance of physical and spiritual disciplines…like shadow boxing, but for the soul.

Comforting Rachel was a pleasure, but it became more difficult for Seth to remain brotherly. He knew he was falling in love. He forced himself to remember that Rachel may be his half-sister and that their relationship could be no more than platonic.

Afternoon hours waned with long periods of time where nothing was said. They both were oblivious to everyone on deck and to the impending danger that awaited them. There were no clouds in the sky and the soft breeze kicked up only small ripples on the water as the *Ladybug* stayed on course for Macau.

*****

General Von paced the floor at his headquarters on Lantau, anxiously awaiting a reply to his cable to Chang aboard the *Ladybug*. He wanted to confirm his conviction as to the identity of the Chinese man Sydney saw in Panama talking to Len Chow; and if Chang were to prove him correct, the Chinese man was the head of the Triad, which was involved in every dirty criminal wrongdoing known to mankind, currently concentrating on gold smuggling in and out of Hong Kong and Macau, and foreign mud (opium) in the Canton area. The general thought he had fled China to seek asylum elsewhere after his near capture in Canton, but he never considered he would go to Panama to hide and carrying on his operation from there.

The general was pleased with Sydney's undercover work in Panama where she discovered that Len Chow was the Triad's local leader in Hong Kong…and best of all that she would be able to identify him. He also knew Andre had told Len Chow how to detect the hollowed timbers bearing the gold, which added more credence to his importance among the smugglers.

"Hot damn!" The general excitedly rejoiced when he read the cable from Chang. "I knew it was General Tso. If his strategy holds

Riding the Tail of the Dragon

true to our previous encounters, he will deploy his men to the warehouse after the timbers are stored and will confiscate the gold from there. He will melt down the twenty-seven-pound bulk bullion into nine-ounce gold bars elsewhere. So far, we haven't had the good fortune to find his main source of operation until after he has vacated it for another location. He's a very clever man."

He turned to Quan Lee saying, "I want you to station your men at various positions along the short distance from the wharf to the warehouse. I'll have my men at the warehouse, and I'm sending Sydney to the ship to stay with Rachel and Seth until this whole thing is over. I'm sure the captain will have a better feeling of safety for his men and his ship if Sydney and the three agents remain on board while the timbers are being transferred from the cargo hold to the trucks. Then I'll want Sydney to identify Len Chow after the fracas is over. Hopefully, it will go in our favor."

Quan Lee agreed and asked, "What about the Legionnaires I've hired?"

"They can stay at the wharf and keep the ship under surveillance. It wouldn't be General Tso's style to rush the ship while docked, so I don't expect any action aboard ship. And, I would just as soon keep the Legionnaires out of the fight, anyway. I'm not too sure I want those vagabonds close to the gold, but I'll use them if I must.

*****

Chang sat on the bridge with Captain Oscarson, cursing his folly for being caught in the middle of this operation. He thought to himself: *Why I not run other way when I see Seth at rickshaw stand. I very dumb. I know bad men following him.* He shook his head and continued his thought: *Uncle not hurt me, maybe, but I not too sure about feng shui.* He resolved: *Okay, I be in wrong place at wrong time.*

The captain startled Chang when he asked, "I see you're shaking your head as if your thoughts are bothering you. Are you worried?"

"Much plenty to worry. I be in hot water with Uncle Tso if he find out I talk to General Von," moaned Chang.

"Don't tell me! General Tso is your Uncle?"

"You betcha," answered Chang.

With a look of disbelief, the captain asked, "How did that happen?"

129

"Easy...I guess. He my honored father's brother. Uncle very great man in War...he get many medals from President Chiang Kai-shek...even Emperor Hirohito honor him. He go down hill fast after War and now he very bad man, but very *rich* bad man."

Captain Oscarson listened with great interest and stated, "General Von has studied General Tso's tactical maneuvers and he is preparing his strategy accordingly. I hope for your sake you won't have to become involved in the fight."

CHAPTER TWENTY-SEVEN

Tensions intensified during the remaining hours of the voyage as the strain took its toll on everyone aboard ship. Captain Oscarson gave a brief talk to his seamen stating there may be a little trouble when the ship docked in Macau, but he did not give an explanation of what to expect, nor did he go into any detail regarding the cargo. He merely asked them to keep alert.

Charlie sat with Seth and Rachel on the storage chest and one-by-one they were joined by Pete, the other agents and the captain. Conversation was sporadic and low key with nothing being discussed of any importance. Their introspective thoughts reflected the temperament of their circumstance. It was still dark when the ship pulled along side the dock in Macau.

Captain Oscarson observed there was only one vessel anchored several hundred yards farther out in the water, and he thought it strange there were no other ships, cargo or otherwise, at the dock. His knowledge of the harbor in Macau was limited, but he assumed there would be more boat activity. He anticipated a delay of at least one day unloading his cargo, but now he planned to contact the harbor officials at daylight for clearance to remain at the dock and unload immediately.

Lights from the dock shimmered across the water illuminating eerie images. Imaginations flared as everyone aboard nervously stood at the railing expecting to see General Von's men on the wharf; but to their disappointment, the entire area was void of movement and sound.

Ten minutes, and an eternity later, they watched a lone figure far down the long pier walking toward the ship. Captain Oscarson thought he recognized the stride of the walker...yes, it was Sydney. A brief greeting was exchanged, but there was no joy in her voice and her countenance expressed the seriousness of her visit. She and the captain quickly retreated to the bridge where she divulged General Von's orders regarding his disbursement of all the men.

Time seemed to stand still and there were many more hours until daylight. No one paid attention to the late hour—no one went to bed—and most remained on deck.

Seth, the three agents and Charlie talked quietly while Rachel curled up at the back of the storage chest to rest after a long, arduous day. Seth did not give his full attention to the conversation as he constantly glanced at Rachel, thinking he must persuade her to return with him to Virginia. The imminent concern for her to inherit the plantation and remain in Virginia had now turned to a personal desire that she become a part of his life. He was dying to call his dad with the good news of finding Rachel and he had many questions regarding her birth that needed to be answered. He wasn't going to let his dad get off the phone before he had an answer to his question—was Rachel his daughter?

There were many questions rolling around in Rachel's head as she lay on the storage chest. She wanted a quiet time to herself to digest the startling information Seth had told her. When she thought about Seth, a rush of emotions rippled through her body awakening feelings she had never experienced. It was a tremor of excitement, which released a good, safe feeling. When he held her hand, it was a gentle touch, but the grip was strong and protective, which she liked. It was a little disquieting, however, that she felt vulnerable and receptive to his touch.

Seth listened to the agents talking and wondered if anyone else noticed how Pete's disposition had changed during the voyage. Where once Pete had shown great interest in his work as the ship's doctor and had administered medical attention to anyone in need, he now was unconcerned, even nonchalant in offering medical advice. He appeared to have lost incentive after Andre died. Seth reasoned Pete's fervent passion to care for Andre served only, upon his death, to turn his human form into a shell where his soul and spirit no longer lived. Seth dwelled upon that thought, remembering Pete's family had been killed in the War and he surmised, perhaps with the death of his patient Andre, he considered himself a failure and now his rudderless life had no meaning.

Friendships were kindled during the long voyage: the captain his mentor and teacher, and Pete his surrogate father. Seth thought: *The tail of the dragon has whipped me all around the world, but with good fortune. I always will be thankful to the positive forces of feng shui for bringing me to Rachel.* It was far more than he had bargained for where he learned life is like an ocean of events, rising

Riding the Tail of the Dragon

and falling with each wave. Whatever the outcome of the confrontation with the gold smugglers, Seth would never regret searching for Rachel.

*****

Was it Seth's imagination or was the only other vessel in the area slowly moving closer to the *Ladybug;* and from Seth's advantage point on the storage chest, he could see men scurrying on its deck. When the three agents turned to see what was captivating Seth's attention, they immediately jumped into action and alerted everyone.

The captain led his sailors to the ship's arsenal returning with a pistol for Seth and Charlie. He quickly sent a cable to General Von on Lantau, but he knew the general had already dispersed his men. It would be up to everyone on the *Ladybug* to hold off the smugglers until help arrived.

This was a moxie move by General Tso, and not consistent with his usual strategy. Only he would have the fortitude to commandeer the *Ladybug* while in port. Captain Oscarson figured General Tso must know General Von's daughter Rachel is aboard and that this coup would be extra delicious where he could command a large ransom for her safe return.

Suddenly, everything went pitch black on the dock. Captain Oscarson called for all the lights on the ship to be turned off, leaving the *Ladybug* surrounded in total darkness.

The marauding vessel pulled closer to the *Ladybug* and its men, all dressed in black with black hoods covering their heads revealing only their eyes, threw grappling hooks connecting the two ships.

Rachel heard the excitement and in an instant was standing at Seth's side. Everyone rushed midship to await the smugglers except Rachel, Seth, Charlie and Pete who stayed at the bow of the ship taking cover behind the storage chest.

Charlie quietly complained, "Feng shui master right. We sail too soon to Macau. We in big trouble."

Rachel whispered, "Do you see something moving on the pier?"

Pete answered, "The whole pier is in darkness, but I'd swear the pier is alive with something."

A volley of shots rang out from the sailors' guns as the smugglers fought their way onto the *Ladybug.* Seth insisted Rachel take cover under a tarpaulin, while he, Pete and Charlie joined in the fight. Their delivered blows to the smugglers were effective, but there were too many of them, and the smugglers were well trained in karate with swift and accurate movements. The few men aboard the *Ladybug* could not stand up to this terrorizing, formidable force.

    Rachel heard the raucous conflict of men fighting for their lives. She had to see what was happening and crawled from beneath the tarpaulin. She gasped a slight screech when she saw the terrible, bloody scene. Her eyes quickly scanned the deck for Seth and she was briefly relieved to see him holding his own with Pete and Charlie fighting beside him. She saw the captain and Sydney on the bridge protecting any advancement by the smugglers to the ship's controls.

    Rachel's attention was drawn to a frenzied commotion where the dock was alive with dark moving figures trying to board the ship. They were the Legionnaires. She ran toward the fighting at midship to lower the rope ladders and the plank. In a matter of seconds, the Legionnaires scrambled to board the ship and swarmed all over the deck reinforcing the strength of the sailors. The smugglers were now far out numbered and the tide of the fighting turned. Within minutes the Legionnaires restrained the smugglers.

    With the swiftness of a panther lunging for its prey, one of the smugglers pounced upon Rachel. His one arm wrapped around her throat while he held a knife in his other hand. The smuggler called to Charlie in Chinese that he would kill the girl if he did not get a safe release for the two of them to return to his boat. Rachel understood what the smuggler had said and screamed. With all her strength she tried to wrestle away, but his tight grip held her locked as his knife came closer to her throat.

    Seth heard her scream and rushed to save her. He balanced, stepping his way on the ship's railing and came up behind the smuggler, knocking him down as he jumped from the railing to the smuggler's back. The knife fell from the smuggler's hand and Rachel quickly moved away. A wild skirmish ensued between Seth and the smuggler for control of the knife.

    Both Pete and Charlie moved instinctively to help Rachel and Seth when they saw the smuggler grappling for the knife. Seth's foot became tangled in a coil of rope and fell to the deck. The smuggler seized the moment to attack Seth while he was down and lunged for him ready to thrust the knife. Pete jumped on the smuggler's back,

Riding the Tail of the Dragon

pulling him off Seth. He fought with a vengeance, releasing all his hostility on the smuggler, and with a fierce pull, yanked the black hood from the smuggler's face. They rolled on the deck, viciously fighting, and once again the smuggler gained control of the knife.

The two backed away from each other, executing a dance-like routine in a circular motion. Each man was keenly capable having taut, sharp reflexes ready to act and react to any advanced movement.

Sydney saw the fight and excitedly yelled to Pete, "It's Len Chow!"

As fast as lightening, Rachel pulled the knife from her belt and slid it across the deck to Pete. Now both men were armed with a knife. The Legionnaires, while keeping the smugglers in check, tried to intervene to stop the fight, but Pete motioned them away—this was a fight to the death.

Each man dashed toward one another committing a suicidal lunge and delivered a death-dealing blow with the strike of a knife. Everyone on board was shouting words of encouragement to his favored victor, eagerly watching to see which man would win.

Len Chow fell immediately while Pete struggled to remain standing, but then succumbed to the mortal strike of Chow's knife to his chest. He fell dead.

*****

Daylight painted a graphic picture of the early morning struggle aboard the *Ladybug;* and even though the actual fighting did not last very long, its intensity was vicious.

Captain Oscarson immediately cabled General Von with news of their victory—thanks to the Legionnaires—and requested approval to unload the timbers as previously arranged.

The captain beamed proudly as he returned to the deck; and with a tone of admiration in his voice called to Seth, "Young man you acquitted yourself quite admirably this morning. You surprised me with your skill in karate."

Seth responded, "Thank you, captain. I didn't realize I'd ever have to use it to save my life. The gym back home where I exercise offers it, and on a fluke I decided to learn it. I'm glad now I did."

The captain added, "I wouldn't have been so concerned for your safety had I known you were skilled in martial arts."

Jeannine Dahlberg

The captain was especially proud of the Legionnaires. He never thought he would rue the day for having called them misfits. It was because of their valor the confrontation with the smugglers was quickly suppressed, which resulted in saving many lives and making it possible to turn over the gold to the proper authorities in Hong Kong.

Quan Lee and his men arrived in good time to assist in the arrest of the smugglers and to take them back to Hong Kong. After they left, the *Ladybug* took on an awesome pallor. A veil of death masked the deck where men had fallen. Those who suffered no injury gave thanks for being alive and paid homage to the dead while watching the medics carry the bodies to shore. Sydney and Seth suffered the tragedy of Pete's death more than anyone else. Sydney felt great remorse for losing a valiant comrade, and Seth reconciled Pete would no longer endure a living death as he would be at peace with his family in heaven.

CHAPTER TWENTY-EIGHT

General Von was extremely pleased with the whole operation dealing with the capture of the smugglers and with confiscating the gold. His deportment of the men to various locations was strategically sound, but the kudos went to the Legionnaires.

He and Rachel sat up most the night while she enthusiastically reported the entire incident to him—not leaving out a single detail of the fight. The story did not fall on deaf ears when Rachel mentioned Seth's name many times and how brave he was. He could easily see by the sparkle in her eyes that she was smitten with the young man.

They discussed at great length her adoption in Paris, which the general immediately confirmed, and he explained in more detail the circumstances involving her mother and her need for Rachel's adoption. He revealed the instant love they had for her as a baby and reaffirmed that the depth of their love continued to deepen with each passing year. He also stated they were a tight threesome where love for one another was the force behind their survival and existence.

Morning light was breaking through the clouds, but she wasn't tired. She still had to talk to her dad about the possibility of her being an heiress to a large tobacco plantation in Virginia. After a long discussion, Rachel started to cry and put her head on his shoulder.

"Dad, I don't want to go to Virginia. I don't want to leave you here on Lantau."

The general urged, "It's time you start a life of your own in a cultural environment begetting your country of birth. Why don't you go to sleep now and we'll talk some more in the morning."

*****

Seth returned to Hong Kong aboard the *Ladybug;* and after the ship docked, he immediately went to the Peninsula Hotel to place a call to his dad in the States. He was so excited he had trouble composing himself while he waited for the call to be placed.

Finally, the phone rang. Seth blurted, "Hello, dad, it's me! You'll never believe the wild ride I've had…and, dad, I found Rachel!"

BillyJoe plunked down on the chair at the kitchen table with a surprised look on his face. He really didn't think Seth would be able to find her; in fact, maybe he really didn't want Seth to find her.

There was a long pause on the phone line and Seth asked, "Dad are you still there?"

"Son, I'm so glad to hear your voice." BillyJoe started to cry. He held the receiver away from his ear and with his other hand, he reached for the bottle of bourbon on the counter behind him and poured a glass. Where once a drink of bourbon gave him strength and support to face his problems, now the bourbon had become a crutch and a weakness, confusing rational thought.

"Dad, dad," called Seth.

"Yes, son, I'm still here. I can't talk, now." BillyJoe said feebly. "I don't feel very well. I'm happy you found Rachel and I'll wire enough money so the two of you can fly home. So long, son."

"Dad, wait, wait! I have to ask you about Rachel. Is she my..." Seth heard the receiver click and the call was disconnected.

*****

Seth had experienced many days filled with anxiety on this whole adventure to find Rachel, but his apprehension for the early morning meeting with General Erik von Horstmann was the most nerve-racking...all other meetings paled by comparison. Just repeating his name inspired awe. His bodacious reputation certainly preceded him, causing everyone who knew him to admire him as a brilliant strategist, a scholar and a gentlemen. Seth felt a little intimidated.

Rachel and the general were comfortably seated in the parlor when Seth arrived. The general stood to welcome Seth with a cordial handshake and Rachel flashed a shy smile as she asked if he wanted a cup of tea. The general liked Seth immediately and expressed deep gratitude for his helping to save Rachel's life.

After pleasantries had been offered, the three discussed the possibility of Rachel returning to Virginia with Seth to confirm if she were, in deed, the heiress to the plantation. The general emphasized that Rachel would regret it for the rest of her life if she didn't explore the truth of her birth. Seth spoke with such enthusiasm for her to fly back to the States with him that the general had to turn his head so neither one could see him smile. It was quite evident Seth was in love with Rachel.

Riding the Tail of the Dragon

Morning hours quickly passed and it was time for Seth to return to the *Ladybug*. It was agreed Seth and Rachel would fly out tomorrow for the States.

Seth whistled a merry tune as he walked the short distance to the dock to be ferried back to the *Ladybug*. He thought: *What can go wrong when I have the positive forces on my side.*

*****

In the afternoon, Seth went to Hong Kong to see Charlie for the last time. He found him at the rickshaw stand smoking an old cigar butt. They walked toward one another in a slow, deliberate step, with a multitude of emotions racing through their heads. The expressions on their faces said it all as they tightly embraced. It was a friendship that had developed quickly, nurtured by circumstances, which create a solid foundation for fraternal trust.

"Charlie, I will always consider you my friend," and with a faltering voice Seth added, "and think of you as a brother I never had."

Charlie stammered, "Boss, you some mighty warrior. We could have had great time together during War. I would trust you with my life. Flying Tigers would have liked you plenty."

Both became very quiet, realizing they may never see one another again.

Charlie continued, "If feng shui agree, I like our paths to cross again some day."

With one last embrace Seth said, "I would like that."

*****

Good-byes were difficult.

Rachel felt cheated of time to spend with her dad. Once it was decided that she go to the States, travel arrangements were quickly made. She felt she was spinning…caught in a whirlwind of fast decisions. Even her emotions were swept up in the whirlwind. How was it possible that she could have strong feelings for Seth when she had only known him for a few days. And yet, it was an intuitive thought that she loved him long before she met him. He fulfilled all her dreams.

General Von regretted he could not spend more time with Rachel. While she was busy packing for her trip to the States, he was spending long hours in meetings with Sydney, Quan Lee and representatives from Britain and France to discuss further actions against the Chinese Triad. Their encounter with Len Chow and the gold smugglers had ended in their favor, but there was much work to be done regarding the opium smuggling in the Canton area. They were planning the take-over of a large shipment of foreign mud in the next few days, and the general made it clear to Quan Lee that he wanted to use the Legionnaires. He wondered if General Tso would be his adversary in this dirty incident as well. General Von vowed that he would get General Tso next time.

General Von assured Quan Lee that he had permitted his cable to British Intelligence to be intercepted regarding their captive, Chang. The Triad would then believe that Chang had been kidnapped and taken to Macau aboard the *Ladybug* against his will. Quan Lee was comforted with this information, as he always had been extremely protective of his best informer, Chang.

*****

Captain Oscarson was extremely happy with the outcome of the delivery of the elm timbers. The gold had been confiscated by the proper authorities and the *Ladybug* sustained no major damage during the fight. His new cargo of bamboo, silk, tea and spices was being loaded into the cargo hold and the ship would be ready to sail the next day. This was turning out to be a successful voyage financially, making it possible to acquire another vessel to add to his fleet.

Seth spent his last night aboard ship talking with the captain. His admiration and respect for the captain spilled over into every topic of discussion. The captain was the smartest man he had ever met…a walking encyclopedia. Viewing the world from the eyes of the captain opened a new dimension to life, making life more vibrant with each learning experience. There were many tense and dangerously exciting times during the past weeks, but Seth would not change anything…with the exception of Pete's death. Seth and the captain agreed it was a happy ending to a long adventure.

CHAPTER TWENTY-NINE

Rachel was apprehensive about the flight to the States not really knowing what to expect. Years ago, she was told the streets were lined with gold, and ice cream parlors were on every corner. True or not, this bit of information held a fascination for her since she was a child, but she was more concerned with the mixed emotions she was experiencing, giving up the security of a loving father to pursue the identity of her biological parents.

Seth peered out the window of the airplane as it left the tarmac to take one last look at Hong Kong. Victoria Harbor was bustling with vessels of all descriptions and he anxiously scanned the harbor for the *Ladybug*. A pang of nostalgia quivered through his body when he located the ship, as he remembered his experiences that turned a boy, not wise in worldly matters, into a young man who had learned to draw upon his resources under desperate situations. He had gained a lifetime of memories during those weeks aboard ship, and he knew he would never forget Captain Oscarson and Pete. Seth resolved his newly found knowledge of ancient Chinese traditions would remain with him for the rest of his life, and he wondered if feng shui would fulfill his destiny that he and Rachel be brought together. He continued to look out the window until Victoria Peak disappeared from view. He was going home.

The airplane seemed to float with big, fluffy, cumulus clouds in the heavenly blue ski, while the two passengers sat side-by-side holding hands, content to be with one another.

Grueling, long hours aboard the airplane drained the two passengers of sleep, but the flight afforded time for conversation where they could explore learning more about one another. They shared memories of their experiences growing up, which made it definitely apparent they were from two very different corners of the world.

After they were well into the flight, Seth withdrew holding Rachel's hand. He knew he was falling in love with her more and more as time went by, but he wanted to restrain his feelings and not make it too obvious to her that he was anything more than a friend.

He wished his dad would have answered his question on the phone. Was she his half-sister?

Rachel became confused by Seth's sudden change in behavior. Maybe she had assumed too much in thinking he could become more than a friend. She hoped he liked her, but she thought it better to be a little reserved and decided to hide her true feelings...if only her eyes would not betray her.

It was late in the evening of the second day of travel that the two young, tired passengers got off the plane happy to be on the ground and anxious to go home.

*****

"Seth, Seth, over here," called BillyJoe, waving his arms high above his head to attract Seth's attention in the busy airport terminal.

"Dad, what are you doing here? I didn't expect you to pick us up," Seth said with a broad smile.

"Well, I knew you would be extremely tired after the long flight and I hated to see you take a taxi to the plantation. I got your cable from Hawaii, when your plane stopped briefly to refuel, giving me your flight number and arrival time, and I thought I would surprise you. I'm sure glad you're home, son." BillyJoe gave him a big, fatherly hug.

BillyJoe turned his attention to Rachel, and with a soft, warm welcome said, "And you must be Rachel. You have the same beautiful eyes like your mother."

Rachel could feel her face redden with warmth. She was blushing again. With a very pretty smile, she cheerfully said, "Mr. Coleman, Seth has told me so much about you." She hesitated a moment to take a long look at BillyJoe and continued, "He is quite proud of his family and speaks with great pride about your dedicated efforts in making this tobacco plantation a successful business. I'm happy to meet you."

BillyJoe listened as she spoke and the tone of her voice also reminded him of her mother, Alice. He realized he was going to have a difficult time in the next few days telling the story about the death of her father, Hank. He tried for many years, with the help of bourbon, to forget how Hank died, but alcohol never provided a lasting escape. He could find no solace. The tragedy of that night will forever shatter his mind with ugly memories, and it will be by his

Riding the Tail of the Dragon

own fortitude, without the bottle, that he must come to grips with his tormented thoughts. But for now, he did not want to appear maudlin and with a quick smile, he suggested, "Let's get your luggage."

BillyJoe was anxious to hear all about Seth's trip, but he thought it best not to discuss it in the automobile while he drove them to the plantation. It was evident his two passengers were very tired and needed sleep. There was no conversation in the car as both closed their eyes and rested during the long drive.

It was late when they rolled into the driveway, and in the dim light of the moon, Seth could see the mansion, prominently positioned on the slope of the hill overlooking the largest lake on the property. It was absolutely beautiful by moonlight, still stately. Seth noticed the heavy green ivy no longer covered the facade, which had draped the mansion in a mysterious aura.

Seth asked, "Dad, have you restored the mansion? It looks great!"

"Yes, I thought it was time to have some outside work done on it. The contractor is coming in a few days and I'm certain Rachel will want to be involved in decorating the interior. The tourist business has been quite lucrative this summer; and I think if the mansion is restored inside and out, business will be better next year. I find it interesting that the tourists are fascinated with the history of the mansion, particularly the story of the ghost of old man Ramsey walking the halls at night. Of course, they enjoy seeing the wine cellar, which still contains one of the largest private collections of premier vintage wines in the country. And the tourists dwell on the macabre story, which our new tour guide embellishes upon, when he takes them down to the dark, damp wine cellar where Hank was killed. Our tour guide sure gives the tourists a lot for their money and his stories get scarier with each telling...and the tourists love it. Of course, it will be up to Rachel if she wants to continue these tours," replied BillyJoe.

Rachel listened to the conversation, but made no comment. There were many questions to be answered before she would offer an opinion.

The Coleman's residence was much larger than Rachel had anticipated for a caretaker's home with the interior design of the rooms being very tastefully decorated...but perhaps a little too

Jeannine Dahlberg

masculine for her taste. She was the first to retire, bidding the others a weary goodnight, and slowly walked to her room…anxious to get a good night's sleep.

    Seth and BillyJoe lingered only a short time in the hallway to express their happiness to see one another and both agreed to wait until morning to discuss the trip. Seth snuggled under the sheets in his bed, completely relaxed, and with a long sigh of relief he thought, *it's great to be home.*

CHAPTER THIRTY

The smell of bacon frying and coffee brewing was too great a temptation to miss by being late for breakfast. Seth bounced down the stairs to a happy, familiar sight to see his dad at the stove cooking his favorite omelet. He quickly walked to the stove and put his arms around his dad's shoulders, bent low over the skillet, smelled the marvelous aroma, and with a broad smile said, "Dad, this is what I really missed on the whole trip."

"I thought you would like some home-cooked food. Let's eat first and talk after breakfast. I know you must be hungry."

Seth did not want to appear that he was wolfing down his breakfast, but he was most anxious to talk to his dad about Rachel.

BillyJoe remarked with a laugh, "My goodness, I think you inhaled your food. I didn't know I was such a good cook."

Finally, breakfast was over and with coffee cups in hand, both decided to sit on the veranda, which provided a panoramic view of the rolling slopes of the plantation. The morning sun cast streams of light through giant oak trees, which surrounded the mansion, coloring the green grass in patches of warm shades of yellow.

Seth was a little nervous as they sat together on a large porch swing, invoking a scene, which was reminiscent of his youth. He waited for his dad to speak first, but, instead, BillyJoe sat quietly, gazing at the mansion. Seth decided to start the conversation with his question about Rachel. He had waited long enough to ask that question. He thought, *now is the time.*

"Dad," Seth stammered, "Is Rachel my half-sister?"

"What?" BillyJoe was stunned by the question. "What makes you think that?"

"Dad, please, just give me a quick answer," Seth pleaded.

It seemed like an eternity passed as BillyJoe sat quietly, rocking in the swing. Seth's heart was pounding like a sledge hammer on concrete and he thought his dad would never answer the question.

"No," was all BillyJoe said, and again quietly repeated the answer, "no".

Seth knew there was more behind the quiet answer, but he decided not to pursue the topic for the present time. He was euphoric

Jeannine Dahlberg

and wanted to shout with joy. His emotions ran rampant with his heart full of love for Rachel, and his great concern that his dad and Alice were lovers conceiving Rachel was obliterated. He spent the next hour telling his dad about the wonderful trip to Europe and his exciting adventure in China. He was thorough in telling the story, reliving each event with the same enthusiasm he had felt during the experience. He spoke with great respect when he mentioned Captain Oscarson, who he believed to be a Renaissance man. He knew he would always honor his teachings, especially what he had learned of life and the universe. He dwelled on the thought and with alacrity explained to his dad that he believed, as the captain had said, that life is a journey to learn about yourself. Nothing is random or accidental and every experience is a learning experience, creating consequences, whether good or bad. The universe is the earth school of your life where everything you do has a meaning and a purpose.

BillyJoe sat quietly listening to his son talk and it became quite apparent to him that Seth admired the captain…and he felt a pang of jealousy. He wondered if Seth would have the same feelings toward him after he unraveled the mysterious story of Hank's death.

BillyJoe was fascinated, but became anxious for his son's safety, when Seth told of his experiences in Hong Kong and the fight with members of the Chinese Triad that followed in Macau. In the short time of a summer vacation, BillyJoe lost a boy and gained a man. Seth had grown in so many different ways to the betterment of his manhood. BillyJoe was very proud of his son.

*****

"Hello, is anybody here," called Rachel as she left the kitchen to search other rooms of the house.

"We're out on the veranda, Rachel," called Seth. "Come on out."

"Wait a minute," BillyJoe offered. "You may want to have a little breakfast before you come outside."

Rachel responded with a fast, "Thanks, Mr. Coleman, but I think I'll wait for lunch before I eat anything. I'm not certain what meal I should be eating anyway as my stomach is still on Hong Kong time. I'm afraid my body rhythm is all out of sync."

Rachel stood on the veranda, gazing at the magnificent view in sight, finding it difficult to believe that she was going to inherit all that she could see, plus many more thousands of acres rich in tobacco fields. The clean, crisp morning air aroused a sensation of happiness as she took in a deep, long breath. She questioned her feeling of happiness to that of betrayal to her home on Lantau with her father. China was very, very far away. How did all this happen?

"Before Seth takes you on a tour of your house and plantation, I want to tell you about your father, Hank," BillyJoe said remorsefully. It was the gnawing distress of guilt that goaded him to speak and he wanted to get it over with quickly.

BillyJoe got off the swing to walk to the column of the veranda where he leaned his back against it as if wanting support for his body. He needed strength and self-assurance for what he was about to say. He looked at Seth and Rachel, who were now sitting together on the swing. He began his story.

"Rachel, you may not want to hear what I'm going to tell you about your father, but I think you should listen to what I have to say. I'd like to try to sugar it up for you, honey, but I can't. He did everything possible in his short time on earth to make life miserable for everyone around him. He was a congenital liar who didn't know right from wrong.

"Miss Patti recognized his mischievous traits when he was a very small boy. When he wasn't in trouble himself, he was conniving to get someone else in trouble...and it didn't make any difference who his victim was. There are a multitude of stories I could tell you, but let it suffice...he was an evil prankster personified! I tried to keep him under control, but he had the Ramsey name and all the power that goes with it. He made my life a living hell.

"His father was blind to everything he did, and I know he resented me for being charged by Miss Patti to look after him. Old man Ramsey was anxious for Hank to grow up to become a man with manly attributes and responsibilities. As years past, the boy grew, but manhood never developed...the childish pranks always prevailed. Mr. Ramsey gave him every opportunity to reach his potential in supervising the plantation, but Hank failed every challenge his dad threw his way...everything was a game to him, which had to be fun...at someone's expense.

"I played a very important role during those frustrating years. Miss Patti insisted I be a shadow to his every move."

BillyJoe stopped at this point, kicking the porch deck with the toe of his shoe and added, "Can you realize what kind of a life I had? It was through self-discipline, willpower, patience, and respect for the Coleman name that I didn't buck this tough chore. Many times I felt like pounding some sense into him. My dad knew how I felt. He would calm my anger by reminding me that the Colemans had always been loyal to the Ramseys, that our place was to serve and that Miss Patti urgently requested that I take care of Hank."

Again BillyJoe paused, cleared the lump in his throat and continued, "Well, I would do anything for Miss Patti. She was like a mother to me...taking the place of the mother I never had."

With a loving softness, he whispered, "and I think she treated me like a son."

"Miss Patti, worried herself into an early grave with grief...regretting she had given birth to a bad seed."

BillyJoe turned to the door to go inside and asked if anyone wanted a cup of coffee. Rachel and Seth did not speak, but shook their head, no. Seth looked tenderly at Rachel as he could see she was bewildered, not knowing what to make of the story. He was about to say something when BillyJoe returned.

"My college days were much better. I finally knew what life was really all about not being shackled to Hank. We both attended the same college; Hank pledged a fraternity and I remained an independent, living in off-campus housing. Often, I would hear stories about his fraternity being in trouble with the alumni or the college officials...mostly when hazing of the pledges became too rough. I always knew Hank was at the center of the problem. I tried to avoid him as much as possible on campus, but that was pretty hard to do. He was extremely popular, especially with the girls, participating in every sporting event. I'll have to admit he was extremely good looking and a lot of fun to be around when he wasn't planning something bad.

"We were in our senior year when we both decided to go home for the biggest event of the year on the plantation. The Ramseys would invite certain friends of European royalty and would host a fox hunt. The lavish splendor provided was breathtaking by ordinary standards. Everyone of wealth and influence wanted to be invited to this party, which would last for three days."

Riding the Tail of the Dragon

BillyJoe sat down on the steps of the veranda, placing his arms on his bent knees and nestled the coffee cup between his hands. It became evident to Rachel and Seth that what they were about to hear of the story was difficult for BillyJoe to tell. Everyone sat quietly for a few minutes.

"The day of the big fox hunt was the beginning of Hank's downward, self-destructing course. There was a magnificent party the evening before and the guests were asked to join in the hunt early the next morning. Everyone was dressed in his finest riding habit and was mounted on our best horses. It was a picture-perfect scene with excitement building when the hound dogs were released to start the chase. The hunt was always one of my favorite times, because I had the opportunity to enjoy myself along with everyone else.

"It had become a ritual between Mr. Ramsey and Hank to race ahead of everyone to jump the small creekbed rather than walk the horses through the gully. I expected this to happen, but I became nervous when I noticed Hank was leading Mr. Ramsey farther down the side of the creek where the creek widens at the entrance to Willow Lake."

BillyJoe switched his attention to Seth and asked, "Son, you remember where that creek comes into Willow Lake, don't you? That's where your grandfather always took you fishing."

Seth nodded, yes, and BillyJoe continued.

"Hank was wild with excitement and I could hear his shrill laugh. Mr. Ramsey continued to race with him, knowing the creek was too wide at that point, but he didn't pull back on his horse's reins...and I was watching closely, hoping he would abort the race.

"The other riders also noticed the two racers were galloping too fast and were quickly approaching the creek. Hank pulled back hard on his reins at the bank of the creek and his horse slid down the short slope, but Mr. Ramsey's horse took a long leap, plunging into the far side of the embankment, throwing Mr. Ramsey off his horse. I can still see him spinning in the air and I can still hear Hank laughing while he sat on his horse safely in the creekbed. Mr. Ramsey died right there of a broken neck.

"Everyone's attention focused on Hank, waiting for him to say something, but he just sat on his horse, looking at his dad on the far side of the creek. To be honest with you, I don't know if Hank was in

Jeannine Dahlberg

shock, felt numb, or was apathetic to the whole accident. I was never able to figure him out. Once again, I rescued Hank by handling the situation as best I could.

"Miss Patti knew what happened, even without being there. She had asked her husband long before to stop the foolish game with Hank, insisting it was too dangerous to jump anywhere along the uneven bank of the creek.

"Everything changed after Mr. Ramsey was killed. There were no more parties; no more laughter in the big house; and Miss Patti withdrew deep into a world of her own, which did not include Hank. She never talked to him after her husband's death.

"After old man Ramsey was buried, my dad's responsibilities increased a great deal. Miss Patti trusted him with every phase of the plantation's operation, which included traveling. At that time, it became necessary for me to learn every facet of supervising this plantation. My dad was a tough task master, drilling the importance of always running this plantation like it were our own, never wavering in our loyalty to the Ramseys. Immediately upon graduation from college, it became necessary for me to oversee its operation when my dad was away."

BillyJoe paced the porch for a short while, conjuring up memories he did not want to remember. He was filled with regret for years wasted on a life-long obligation to the Ramsey plantation. He never was able to realize his dream of becoming a civil engineer, traveling all over the world building beautiful bridges.. and his failed marriage broke his spirit. He believed for whatever greater plan there was for him, he was to remain on the Ramsey plantation. He was proud of one accomplishment in his life, however, and that was being a father to Seth. He stopped pacing the porch to give a tender, loving look at Seth and he continued...

"Seth, your mom and I married immediately after graduation. I had promised her that we would live a life together, traveling around the world and living for only a short time at any given location while I built beautiful bridges."

BillyJoe gazed longingly across the landscape as if he were trying to see the other side of the world and regrettably said, "Oh, the fickle dreams of youth."

With a stronger voice he said, "Your mom was happy living on the plantation for awhile, but I could see the daily routine started to bore her. She wanted the things I had promised her and when you were about two years old, she decided to leave us. She told me she wanted to start living."

BillyJoe turned his attention to Rachel saying, "Rachel, your mother was a beautiful woman who could have had any man on campus she wanted. I think they were all in love with her. Why she chose to marry Hank still remains a mystery to me. They married a couple of years later after graduation and moved into the big house with Miss Patti. I think, maybe, Alice probably had a few happy months, but things deteriorated quickly after Hank started drinking.

"When situations got out of control, Alice would come here for a few hours in the late afternoon to play with Seth. She was happy here and when the hour came and she thought she had better return to the big house, she hated to go. I started rearranging my time in the office so I could spend an hour or two talking with her. I tried to hide my feelings, but I knew I had fallen in love with her. We would talk about everything and anything. After awhile, she took me into her confidence and started unloading the problems she was having with Hank. I became very concerned for her safety when she told me Hank was getting violent after drinking too much wine. I asked if she had mentioned Hank's behavior to Miss Patti, but she said, no, that she rarely saw her; and when she did, Miss Patti would indicate that she did not want to talk about it."

BillyJoe hesitated to go on with the story. He felt he was suffocating with emotions that had been stifled for years. He asked Rachel and Seth if he could get them something from the kitchen as he needed another cup of coffee. They both agreed, no; and showed that they were eager to hear the rest of the story.

BillyJoe returned to the kitchen and immediately walked to the cabinet, grabbed the bourbon bottle and twisted off the cap. He was ready to pour the bourbon in a glass when he put the bottle down. A raging battle was going on in his head…should he or shouldn't he have a much needed shot of bourbon. His hands started to tremble in anticipation of a drink. He hit the counter top with his fist and screwed the cap back on the bottle. He knew he needed a clear head to continue the story. He pushed open the screen door with such force Rachel and Seth moved quickly to separate, but Seth continued to rest his arm around her shoulders as the two sat on the swing waiting for BillyJoe to continue.

"Dad, where's your coffee," Seth asked, being alert to his dad's alcohol failings.

BillyJoe mumbled, "Oh, I've had enough coffee already this morning. It gives me the jitters, anyway."

The only audible sound that was heard over the next few minutes was the quiet squeak of the swing as the two slowly pushed it back and forth in a rhythmic motion. BillyJoe was visibly agitated as he stood before Rachel and Seth with his hands trembling. He jammed his hands in his pant's pockets and again leaned against the porch column for support; and in a low, whispered tone he began the story.

"Rachel, your mother did everything she could to restore an atmosphere of happiness in the big house. She was loved by all the servants; some admired her, knowing what kind of a life she had to endure as Hank's wife, but all felt pity for her.

"I fault Miss Patti during this time because she did nothing to help Alice feel comfortable; in fact, she spent most of her days in her bedroom. Many evenings, I could hear Alice crying and Hank yelling in an alcoholic diatribe maliciously criticizing her for one thing or another. I would look out the kitchen window where I could watch what was happening and I always noticed Miss Patti walking back and forth on her bedroom balcony. She could hear the arguments more clearly than I.

"One Sunday afternoon, when Alice had come over to play with Seth, she told me that she was pregnant. She looked absolutely beautiful, and for the first time in quite awhile, she was genuinely happy. It was no pretense. She told me that she hoped the baby would bind the marriage and bring her and Hank closer together. A pang of jealously ran through me. I wished it were my child she was having. I would have given anything to take her in my arms, smother her with kisses and tell her I loved her. Hank didn't deserve her.

"Well, her idea worked in reverse. Shortly after midnight, I was awakened by sharp, piercing screams. It was Alice. Her first calls were for help and then she started calling, 'BillyJoe,' BillyJoe.' Her voice was so loud and clear that I thought she was standing outside my bedroom window. I flew out of bed and rushed to see what was

Riding the Tail of the Dragon

happening. I couldn't believe my eyes. Hank was dragging Alice across the yard, yelling at the top of his lungs that he didn't want to have a kid. I saw a light go on in Miss Patti's bedroom and she witnessed the terrible incident from her window.

"I quickly dressed and ran to the big house. A light from the den was streaming through the half-closed door. I stood for a moment…not believing the scene before me. Alice was cowering in the corner of the room, crying and holding her stomach as if cradling her unborn baby. Hank was at the desk trying to shake out more wine from an empty decanter and futilely looking around the room for more wine. Miss Patti was pleading with Hank to tend to his wife to see if she was hurt. Hank paid her no attention. Miss Patti picked up an empty wine bottle and struck him hard over the head. He staggered a moment from the blow then spun around, and with blurred, crazy eyes, he shoved Miss Patti across the room. Hank was out of control. Both women I dearly loved were crying on the floor and Hank was staggering out the doorway to find more wine. I ran to Alice and Miss Patti to make certain they were all right. I tried to hold my emotions in check and remain rational, but all the years of hatred for this man now consumed my whole being. I could feel the hot rush of blood in my head as I went after Hank. I wanted to kill him.

"I knew he was going to head for the wine cellar. I stood at the top of the stairs and watched that pathetic figure stumble down each step. The dimly lit cellar cast grotesque shadows on the walls and I continued to watch as Hank staggered to the far end of the cellar where he tried to climb up the wine rack to reach a particular vintage wine. I recalled how many times Hank had been warned by the servants not to climb the rack as it could easily tumble down on him. I continued to watch as he took one precarious step after another to reach the top. I could feel a disaster was in the making and I just stood there and did nothing. Within minutes, the whole wine rack came crashing to the floor with Hank under it. Broken wine bottles were everywhere and I could hear Hank moaning. I was in no hurry to rescue him. Hell! I savored every moment of his agony. I wanted him to suffer as he had made me suffer all the years I had to look after him, and I wanted him to suffer for all the people he had hurt. My first thought was to let him lie there until morning and let the servants find him. I guess it was my conscience or perhaps years of disciplined training to keep Hank out of harm's way that instigated my first move, once again, to help him out of trouble. I waited for him to stop moaning and then I slowly stepped forward to remove the wine rack. It wouldn't budge. I found a long plank, placed it over a beer keg and used it as leverage to raise the wine rack...it worked. I gasped when I saw Hank's body covered in blood and a large piece of broken glass from a wine bottle protruding from his neck. He was dead.

"I sat there for quite a long time looking at this spoiled, miserable human being. All his life he was like a freight train running out of control heading for an accident. I thought of all the misery he had caused everyone and, yet, I felt sorry for him."

BillyJoe stopped at this point in the story, kicked the toe of his shoe on the porch deck and continued. "I could have prevented his accident...all I had to do was pull him down from the wine rack. It's ironic. He was buried under what he had come to love most in the world...alcohol."

BillyJoe coughed away a large lump in his throat and said, "Your mother didn't want to live on the plantation any longer as everything reminded her of Hank. She wanted to get far away from here to try to find happiness. I almost think this plantation is a curse to women. There hasn't been a woman who has found happiness living here in several generations."

Tears started to roll down Rachel's cheeks as Seth moved closer to comfort her, and BillyJoe continued.

"Rachel, honey, I'm sorry for telling you this story about your daddy. Years of pent-up hatred reached its boiling point that night. My shame is I delighted in watching him climb the wine rack, knowing that it would fall on him. The crazy thing is: the first time I didn't rescue him from some disastrous incident, he's killed.

"I'm not proud of myself and your daddy's horrible death lives with me every day of my life. The police investigated and called it an accident...which it was; but in my heart, I will always know I could have prevented his death. I have never told anyone that I quietly stood by and did nothing to help Hank...and I'll have to live with that."

BillyJoe stood taller and moved forward from the column and with more strength in his voice he said, "By telling you the truth, I feel I have purged my soul from harboring guilt for my slothful action to help Hank and I'm experiencing an inner peace that I haven't known for many years. Maybe, happiness will not elude me any longer."

He stepped to the swing where the two sat and lovingly placed his hand on Rachel's shoulder with an emotional warmth that permeated Rachel's comprehension…and she understood his dilemma. He stood for a long time looking down at Rachel…their eyes holding fast with understanding for each other's complex, emotional reaction.

Dazed and confused, Rachel stared at the big house, visualizing the tragic accident of her father's death. Her thoughts were in a rational torpor with all the details of the stories swimming around in her head. Exploring the identity of her biological parents appealed to her desire to know the truth of her birth; but upon hearing the truth, the emotional trauma was almost more than she could bear. Perhaps, it would have been better if she had not learned anything about her real father. BillyJoe needed to cleanse his soul of the burden of truth, but the unflattering characterization revealed to her about her father rested heavily with her. She leaned over to Seth and gently placed her head on his shoulder, wondering if she did the right thing by returning with him to the States.

CHAPTER THIRTY-ONE

How do I really want to live my life? was the question that confronted Rachel. The last few weeks were delightful; being introduced to the servants, moving into the big house; touring the plantation and meeting a few of the key personnel. BillyJoe was eager to make her feel at home and treated her like a daughter. And Seth…Seth was very attentive openly displaying his affection for her. And, yet, she wondered *why am I not happy?* She and BillyJoe had traveled to the courthouse to satisfy legal records that she was born Rachel Ramsey and was entitled to inherit the plantation, which pleased BillyJoe. She thought, *everything is great! I feel blessed to have fallen into this nirvana.*

She continued to sit in her big, beautifully decorated bedroom gazing out the window, which overlooked the lake and tears welled in her eyes. In her hand she held a picture of her mother and father, which was taken when she was a small girl in Germany. Her mother wore a designer-fashion gown and her father cut a striking figure in his general's uniform. Those were days of affluence and she still had vivid recollections of her life at that time. She reflected upon her life in the orphanage in Paris with her mother; the hectic flight with the general to Macau…so many memories…so many difficult, dangerous times…so much love nurtured out of adversity.

Her reverie was broken when she heard a knock at the door. It was the maid announcing that Seth was downstairs in the atrium. She quickly wiped the tears from her eyes and ran down the stairs to greet him.

"Oh, Seth, I'm so glad you're here." Rachel rushed into his arms and they kissed passionately.

"You've been crying. What's the matter?" Seth asked.

"I'm all mixed up. I don't know what I want." She looked tenderly at Seth with tears again filling her eyes. "I love you so much…it hurts."

Seth held her tightly and they kissed. He waited for her to say what was on her mind while fearing to hear what she was going to say.

"Seth, I feel as if I'm caught up in a whirlwind. My emotions are frazzled and my thoughts keep drifting back to Lantau and my father. I know I should be happy here...I have everything a girl could want...even my new name, Rachel Ramsey, has a nice ring to it."

"Rachel, you can't go back to Lantau. I'd be lost without you, now. The name Rachel Coleman has a better ring to it." He hastened to add, "Will you marry me?"

She clung tightly to Seth with tears streaming down her cheeks. She was in the arms of the man she loved, but she hesitated to answer. *Yes, I want to marry Seth; no, I don't want to live in the States* were among many vacillating thoughts racing through her head.

Finally, she whispered in his ear, "Please don't ask me to marry you, now. I have to find out where I belong."

Seth pulled away so he could look into her eyes and lovingly said, "You belong with me."

Together, holding hands, the two lovers slowly strolled into the garden to enjoy the crisp, cool air. The morning sun painted the landscape in rich fall colors of red and gold framing steam rising from the lake. Meadow larks contributed a lilting song to a pristine picture...perfect for young lovers.

Rachel broke the silence, "How can I be so happy and so miserable at the same time. The servants, the office staff, everyone has made me feel comfortable and at home. And your father is a sweet, compassionate man. I could never harbor any ill feelings toward him." She spoke slowly and deliberately, "We are from opposite ends of the world. We grew up living vastly different experiences in extremely diverse cultures.

"I'm a very lucky girl, I know, inheriting a beautiful, prosperous plantation and falling in love...all in the course of a few weeks. It's happened all too quickly.

"Seth, I've lived through danger, mystery and intrigue, and a big part of my life, now, is the children in the orphanage on Lantau. I'm afraid to live on the plantation as I probably would become bored like so many women before me. If you believe in feng shui, there may be forces in the big house that adversely act upon a woman's happiness. I'm not superstitious, but there are times when I believe feng shui can control our destiny."

Seth assertively said. "I received a notice from the draft board a few days ago and I have to report for duty day after tomorrow. Many of my friends have already been called up for either the army or the marines and it looks like we're going to Korea. I hesitated to tell you sooner because I had to work out a few details in my own mind. We could get married before I'm sent overseas. You don't have to live on the plantation. My dad has managed quite well these past years…in fact, he's increased productivity and profitability. I think he's really content to live on the plantation although he may not always admit to it. He knows no other life. Rachel, don't you see, we could build a new life together and create our own world."

Rachel could easily see Seth was excited with the idea. She tried to choose her words carefully. "I guess what I'm trying to say is: I need time to digest everything that has turned my life upside down. To choose right now, right here, this morning, what will affect me for the rest of my life, is a decision of such magnitude, I can't handle it." She threw her arms wide in total frustration, looking to Seth for guidance and implored, "Please be patient with me."

*****

BillyJoe sat on Seth's bed remembering how many times over the years he had watched him pack his suitcases. Leaving home for summer camp or college was different, though, this time he was packing to go to war. The full impact of Seth's leaving hit him at breakfast when he realized Seth was the first Coleman in a long line of family men to leave the plantation for any reason. After his military duty, there would be his professional career that would necessitate that he leave home…so Seth was packing for a lifetime.

"Dad, why so gloomy?" Seth jokingly asked. "You're finally getting rid of me."

"I'm sitting here thinking of all the good times we've had over the years—interrupted by a few difficult times—and I hope we will always keep this father/son thing going. It's been just the two of us for many years and I'm going to have to adjust to rattlin' around this big place all by myself."

"Dad, there's something I want to talk to you about." Seth sat down on the bed next to his dad. "I've asked Rachel to marry me."

"That's no shock to me," BillyJoe said laughingly. "I've noticed the way you two look at one another. When's the big day?"

"Rachel's coming over in a few minutes..." Seth let the sentence trail off when he heard her call from downstairs.

Rachel was pacing the floor by the front door with a serious expression on her face, which worried the two as they came down the stairs.

"I called my father this morning," Rachel began, "and BillyJoe I'd like to talk about something that has been on my mind the past few days."

BillyJoe led Rachel and Seth into the kitchen, suggesting they would be more comfortable talking over a cup of coffee.

Rachel looked affectionately at Seth for a moment as if soliciting reassurance for what she was going to say. "BillyJoe," there was a long pause while she searched for the right words.

"When I was a little girl living in an orphanage in Paris during the War, I used to dream I was a princess living in a big castle with lots of servants, wearing beautiful dresses and eating from long tables covered with food. When I grew older living in Macau, I dreamed of being a secret agent working under extremely dangerous situations to free the Orient of drug traffickers. And when I lived on the island of Lantau, I dreamed of saving all the abandoned children in China, showing them love, giving them decent clothing and providing milk and food."

Rachel bowed her head and coyly said, "Seth has appeared in quite a few of my dreams lately; I just wasn't able to give him a face until I met him in Hong Kong. He has been my hero in a fantasy world of dreams and I didn't dare to think I could find him in my real world. He fulfills my every expectation and desire and I deeply love him."

BillyJoe listened attentively, but wondered where this story was going when she continued.

"My dad agreed to my suggestion: I want to make you a full partner...splitting everything fifty-fifty. Realistically, the plantation and business have been yours since Miss Patti died. You have run this whole operation by yourself, increasing the value of the business to a grandiose scale and I want to reward your loyalty. For generations, the Colemans have taken care of the Ramseys and, now, I want to show you our appreciation.

Jeannine Dahlberg

"The whole idea of my being a Ramsey is new to me." She paused to fidget with her neck scarf and said, "I really don't deserve all this. I'm from another world...my heart and the life I have come to love are in China."

"I'm going to contact our lawyer 'and ask him to draw up the papers immediately and we will call the business operation, Ram-Co."

BillyJoe was overwhelmed with gratitude not really knowing how to accept it. Thanks was too simple a word to express for generations of devoted service that contributed to a comfortable livelihood for him and for all the Colemans who preceded him.

Before he could say anything, Rachel continued, "I want to give all our employees who have worked for us for ten years or more a bonus to compensate them for their continued loyalty to the plantation since Miss Patti died."

BillyJoe said with sincerity, "Your generosity is beyond belief. I'm speechless. Please know that thanks comes from the bottom of my heart." BillyJoe was moved to tears; he pulled a handkerchief from his pocket and wiped his eyes.

Rachel took Seth's hand and suggested they walk around the lake.

BillyJoe sat for some time not fully comprehending what he had just heard. The reality of being a co-owner would take a few days for its impact to take effect. He started to reach for the bottle of bourbon from the cabinet, but with a strong conviction of thought, he knew it was time to quit drinking. He said to himself, *and I'm going to quit cold turkey.* He picked up the bottle and poured its contents into the sink.

*****

Large, fluffy white cumulus clouds slowly drifted across a bright blue sky as the two meandered to their favorite spot at the edge of the lake. Each simultaneously picked up a smooth, flat pebble and skipped it across the water to see how many jumps the pebble would make. It was a little game they had played several times with the winner receiving the same number of kisses as jumps made by the pebble. They were in love and each knew the time was fast approaching when serious decisions had to be made.

"Seth," Rachel began, "I've decided to return to China. The general says the Korean conflict is expanding to war proportions and

Riding the Tail of the Dragon

the people in China are feeling its repercussion. The orphanage is beginning to fill again with children seeking refuge. I feel I'm needed at home."

It was tough for Seth to listen to these words as a few days ago everything was different. Being drafted into the army drastically changed all plans. His ambition to become an architect would be put on hold as well as their plans to marry.

"Rachel, the early morning news report on the radio stated our troops are pushing farther north in Korea. Things don't look very good."

"How can this be happening to me," Rachel angrily cried. "I lived through one horrible war and now I have to endure being separated from you because of the Korean War. It's not fair!"

"I received a letter from one of my buddies the other day and he said the army is giving him a rest and recuperation leave to Japan for a few days. When it's my time for R-and-R, maybe we could meet in Japan. It wouldn't be a long flight for you to make from Hong Kong and we could spend a few days together. Please don't cry, Rachel. You'll see. The time will pass quickly and before you know it, the war will be over and I'll be out of the service."

His words of encouragement definitely helped to bolster his spirits, too.

"No matter where the army sends me in this big world, when it's ten o'clock at night in Hong Kong, I will think of you and tell you I love you."

Rachel enthusiastically said, "Oh, Seth, that's such a great idea! At ten o'clock I will do the same. Our spirits will communicate even though we cannot be together physically."

He pulled her closer to him and cupped his hands around her face; she closed her eyes and they passionately kissed.

Seth looked upward to heaven in prayerful thought and again noticed the big clouds.

"Did you ever try to find something in clouds…a ship, an animal, an ogre?"

"Many times," she replied.

Seth jumped to his feet and with excitement in his voice called, "Look! It's a dragon…up there in that big cloud next to the three smaller clouds!"

Jeannine Dahlberg

"I see it! I see it!" She joyfully cried.

"Oh, Rachel, that's a good sign…a symbol of harmony and well-being. Our love is a positive emotion, which we will cultivate, and it will give us strength to endure what lies ahead of us. It's not for us to understand, now; but for purposes beyond our control, we are to be separated at this time. All experiences have a meaning. We must not lose heart. Our creative, loving spirits will appease feng shui and the power of the benevolent dragon will intercede against any adversities. It may take awhile…and then together we will find happiness riding the tail of the dragon."

ABOUT THE AUTHOR

Jeannine Dahlberg combines her love and knowledge of foreign travel with her ability and experience as a writer to tell the story *Riding the Tail of the Dragon* with passion. She lives in St. Louis, Missouri.

Printed in the United States
725200003B